T5-CWL-544

THE HERITAGE OF DEDLOW
MARSH AND OTHER TALES

THE HERITAGE OF DEDLOW
MARSH AND OTHER TALES

BY

BRET HARTE

Short Story Index Reprint Series

BOOKS FOR LIBRARIES PRESS
FREEPORT, NEW YORK

First Published 1889
Reprinted 1970

STANDARD BOOK NUMBER:
8369-3518-7

LIBRARY OF CONGRESS CATALOG CARD NUMBER:
76-121561

PRINTED IN THE UNITED STATES OF AMERICA

CONTENTS.

---•---

THE HERITAGE OF DEDLOW MARSH.

———◆———

I.

THE sun was going down on the Dedlow
Marshes. The tide was following i⁺ fast as
if to meet the reddening lines of sky and
water in the west, leaving the foreground to
grow blacker and blacker every moment, and
to bring out in startling contrast the few
half-filled and half-lit pools left behind and
forgotten. The strong breath of the Pacific
fanning their surfaces at times kindled them
into a dull glow like dying embers. A
cloud of sand-pipers rose white from one of
the nearer lagoons, swept in a long eddying
ring against the sunset, and became a black
and dropping rain to seaward. The long
sinuous line of channel, fading with the light
and ebbing with the tide, began to give off
here and there light puffs of gray-winged
birds like sudden exhalations. High in the
darkening sky the long arrow-headed lines

of geese and 'brant' pointed towards the upland. As the light grew more uncertain the
air at times was filled with the rush of view-
less and melancholy wings, or became plain-
tive with far-off cries and lamentations. As
the Marshes grew blacker the far-scattered
tussocks and accretions on its level surface
began to loom in exaggerated outline, and
two human figures, suddenly emerging erect
on the bank of the hidden channel, assumed
the proportion of giants.

When they had moored their unseen boat,
they still appeared for some moments to be
moving vaguely and aimlessly round the
spot where they had disembarked. But as
the eye became familiar with the darkness it
was seen that they were really advancing inland, yet with a slowness of progression and
deviousness of course that appeared inexplicable to the distant spectator. Presently it
was evident that this seemingly even, vast,
black expanse was traversed and intersected
by inky creeks and small channels, which
made human progression difficult and dangerous. As they appeared nearer and their
figures took more natural proportions, it
could be seen that each carried a gun; that
one was a young girl, although dressed so

like her companion in shaggy pea-jacket and
sou'wester as to be scarcely distinguished
from him above the short skirt that came
halfway down her high india-rubber fishing-
boots. By the time they had reached firmer
ground, and turned to look back at the sunset, it could be also seen that the likeness
between their faces was remarkable. Both,
had crisp, black, tightly curling hair; both
had dark eyes and heavy eyebrows; both
had quick vivid complexions, slightly heightened by the sea and wind. But more striking than their similarity of coloring was the
likeness of expression and bearing. Both
wore the same air of picturesque energy;
both bore themselves with a like graceful
effrontery and self-possession.

The young man continued his way. The
young girl lingered for a moment looking
seaward, with her small brown hand lifted
to shade her eyes, — a precaution which her
heavy eyebrows and long lashes seemed to
render utterly gratuitous.

"Come along, Mag. What are ye waitin'
for?" said the young man impatiently.

"Nothin'. Lookin' at that boat from the
Fort." Her clear eyes were watching a small
skiff, invisible to less keen-sighted observers,

aground upon a flat near the mouth of the channel. " Them chaps will have a high ole time gunnin' thar, stuck in the mud, and the tide goin' out like sixty ! "

" Never you mind the sodgers," returned her companion, aggressively, " they kin take care o' their own precious skins, or Uncle Sam will do it for 'em, I reckon. Anyhow the people — that's you and me, Mag — is expected to pay for their foolishness. That's what they're sent yer for. Ye oughter to be satisfied with that," he added with deep sarcasm.

" I reckon they ain't expected to do much off o' dry land, and they can't help bein' queer on the water," returned the young girl with a reflecting sense of justice.

" Then they ain't no call to go gunnin', and wastin' Guv'nment powder on ducks instead o' Injins."

" Thet's so," said the girl thoughtfully. " Wonder ef Guv'nment pays for them frocks the Kernel's girls went cavortin' round Logport in last Sunday — they looked like a cirkis."

" Like ez not the old Kernel gets it outer contracts — one way or another. *We* pay for it all the same," he added gloomily.

" Jest the same ez if they were *my* clothes,"
said the girl, with a quick, fiery, little laugh,
" ain't it? Wonder how they 'd like my
sayin' that to 'em when they was prancin'
round, eh, Jim ? "

But her companion was evidently unpre-
pared for this sweeping feminine deduction,
and stopped it with masculine promptitude.

" Look yer — instead o' botherin' your
head about what the Fort girls wear, you 'd
better trot along a little more lively. It 's
late enough now."

" But these darned boots hurt like pizen,"
said the girl, limping. " They swallowed a
lot o' water over the tops while I was wadin'
down there, and my feet go swashin' around
like in a churn every step."

" Lean on me, baby," he returned, passing
his arm around her waist, and dropping her
head smartly on his shoulder. " Thar ! " The
act was brotherly and slightly contemptuous,
but it was sufficient to at once establish their
kinship.

They continued on thus for some moments
in silence, the girl, I fear, after the fashion
of her sex, taking the fullest advantage of
this slightly sentimental and caressing attitude. They were moving now along the

edge of the Marsh, parallel with the line of rapidly fading horizon, following some trail only known to their keen youthful eyes. It was growing darker and darker. The cries of the sea-birds had ceased ; even the call of a belated plover had died away inland ; the hush of death lay over the black funereal pall of marsh at their side. The tide had run out with the day. Even the sea-breeze had lulled in this dead slack-water of all nature, as if waiting outside the bar with the ocean, the stars, and the night.

Suddenly the girl stopped and halted her companion. The faint far sound of a bugle broke the silence, if the idea of interruption could have been conveyed by the two or three exquisite vibrations that seemed born of that silence itself, and to fade and die in it without break or discord. Yet it was only the ' retreat ' call from the Fort two miles distant and invisible.

The young girl's face had become irra-diated, and her small mouth half opened as she listened. " Do you know, Jim," she said with a confidential sigh, " I allus put words to that when I hear it — it's so pow'ful pretty. It allus goes to me like this : ' Goes the day, Far away, With the light, And the night Comes along — Comes along — Comes along — Like a-a so-o-ong.'" She here lifted her voice, a sweet, fresh, boyish contralto, in such an admirable imitation of the bugle that her brother, after the fashion of more select auditors, was for a moment quite convinced that the words meant something. Nevertheless, as a brother, it was his duty to crush this weakness. "Yes; and it says: 'Shut your head, Go to bed,'" he returned irascibly; "and *you'd* better come along, if we're goin' to hev any supper. There's Yeller Bob hez got ahead of us over there with the game already."

The girl glanced towards a slouching burdened figure that now appeared to be preceding them, straightened herself suddenly, and then looked attentively towards the Marsh.

"Not the sodgers again?" said her brother impatiently.

"No," she said quickly; "but if that don't beat anythin'! I'd hev sworn, Jim, that Yeller Bob was somewhere behind us. I saw him only jest now when 'Taps' sounded, somewhere over thar." She pointed with a half-uneasy expression in quite another direction from that in which the slouching Yellow Bob had just loomed.

" Tell ye what, Mag, makin' poetry outer bugle calls hez kinder muddled ye. *That's* Yeller Bob ahead, and ye orter know Injins well enuff by this time to remember that they allus crop up jest when ye don't expect them. And there's the bresh jest afore us. Come ! "

The ' bresh,' or low bushes, was really a line of stunted willows and alders that seemed to have . gradually sunk into the level of the plain, but increased in size farther inland, until they grew to the height and density of a wood. Seen from the channel it had the appearance of a green cape or promontory thrust upon the Marsh. Passing through its tangled recesses, with the aid of some unerring instinct, the two companions emerged upon another and much larger level that seemed as illimitable as the bay. The strong breath of the ocean lying just beyond the bar and estuary they were now facing came to them salt and humid as another tide. The nearer expanse of open water reflected the after-glow, and lightened the landscape. And between the two wayfarers and the horizon rose, bleak and startling, the strange outlines of their home.

At first it seemed a ruined colonnade of

many pillars, whose base and pediment were
buried in the earth, supporting a long paral-
lelogram of entablature and cornices. But a
second glance showed it to be a one-storied
building, upheld above the Marsh by num-
berless piles placed at regular distances;
some of them sunken or inclined from the
perpendicular, increasing the first illusion.
Between these pillars, which permitted a free
circulation of air, and, at extraordinary tides,
even the waters of the bay itself, the level
waste of marsh, the bay, the surges of the
bar, and finally the red horizon line, were
distinctly visible. A railed gallery or platform, supported also on piles, and reached
by steps from the Marsh, ran around the
building, and gave access to the several rooms
and offices.

But if the appearance of this lacustrine
and amphibious dwelling was striking, and
not without a certain rude and massive
grandeur, its grounds and possessions,
through which the brother and sister were
still picking their way, were even more grotesque and remarkable. Over a space of
half a dozen acres the flotsam and jetsam of
years of tidal offerings were collected, and
even guarded with a certain care. The

blackened hulks of huge uprooted trees, scarcely distinguishable from the fragments of genuine wrecks beside them, were securely fastened by chains to stakes and piles driven in the marsh, while heaps of broken and disjointed bamboo orange crates, held together by ropes of fibre, glistened like ligamented bones heaped in the dead valley. Masts, spars, fragments of shell-encrusted boats, binnacles, round-houses and galleys, and part of the after-deck of a coasting schooner, had ceased their wanderings and found rest in this vast cemetery of the sea. The legend on a wheel-house, the lettering on a stern or bow, served for mortuary inscription. Wailed over by the trade winds, mourned by lamenting sea-birds, once every year the tide visited its lost dead and left them wet with its tears:

To such a spot and its surroundings the atmosphere of tradition and mystery was not wanting. Six years ago Boone Culpepper had built the house, and brought to it his wife — variously believed to be a gypsy, a Mexican, a bright mulatto, a Digger Indian, a South Sea princess from Tahiti, somebody else's wife — but in reality a little Creole woman from New Orleans, with whom he had contracted a marriage, with other

gambling debts, during a winter's vacation
from his home in Virginia. At the end of
two years she had died, succumbing, as dif-
ferently stated, from perpetual wet feet, or
the misanthropic idiosyncrasies of her husband, and leaving behind her a girl of
twelve and a boy of sixteen to console him.
How futile was this bequest may be guessed
from a brief summary of Mr. Culpepper's
peculiarities. They were the development
of a singular form of aggrandizement and
misanthropy. On his arrival at Logport he
had bought a part of the apparently value-
less Dedlow Marsh from the Government at
less than a dollar an acre, continuing his
singular investment year by year until he
was the owner of three leagues of amphibious domain. It was then discovered that
this property carried with it the *water front*
of divers valuable and convenient sites for
manufactures and the commercial ports of a
noble bay, as well as the natural *embarcade-
ros* of some 'lumbering' inland settlements.
Boone Culpepper would not sell. Boone
Culpepper would not rent or lease. Boone
Culpepper held an invincible blockade of his
neighbors, and the progress and improvement he despised — granting only, after a

royal fashion, occasional license, revocable at pleasure, in the shape of tolls, which amply supported him, with the game he shot in his kingfisher's eyrie on the Marsh. Even the Government that had made him powerful was obliged to 'condemn' a part of his property at an equitable price for the purposes of Fort Redwood, in which the adjacent town of Logport shared. And Boone Culpepper, unable to resist the act, refused to receive the compensation or quit-claim the town. In his scant intercourse with his neighbors he always alluded to it as his own, showed it to his children as part of their strange inheritance, and exhibited the starry flag that floated from the Fort as a flaunting insult to their youthful eyes. Hated, feared, and superstitiously shunned by some, regarded as a madman by others, familiarly known as 'The Kingfisher of Dedlow,' Boone Culpepper was one day found floating dead in his skiff, with a charge of shot through his head and shoulders. The shot-gun lying at his feet at the bottom of the boat indicated the 'accident' as recorded in the verdict of the coroner's jury — but not by the people. A thousand rumors of murder or suicide prevailed, but always with

the universal rider, ' Served him right.' So
invincible was this feeling that but few
attended his last rites, which took place at
high water. The delay of the officiating
clergyman lost the tide; the homely cata-
falque — his own boat — was left aground
on the Marsh, and deserted by all mourners
except the two children. Whatever he had
instilled into them by precept and example,
whatever took place that night in their
lonely watch by his bier on the black marshes,
it was certain that those who confidently
looked for any change in the administration
of the Dedlow Marsh were cruelly mistaken.
The old Kingfisher was dead, but he had
left in the nest two young birds, more beautiful and graceful, it was true, yet as fierce
and tenacious of beak and talon.

II.

ARRIVING at the house, the young people
ascended the outer flight of wooden steps,
which bore an odd likeness to the compan-
ion-way of a vessel, and the gallery, or
' deck,' as it was called — where a number
of nets, floats, and buoys thrown over the
railing completed the nautical resemblance.

This part of the building was evidently devoted to kitchen, dining-room, and domestic offices; the principal room in the centre serving as hall or living-room, and communicating on the other side with two sleeping apartments. It was of considerable size, with heavy lateral beams across the ceiling — built, like the rest of the house, with a certain maritime strength — and looked not unlike a saloon cabin. An enormous open Franklin stove between the windows, as large as a chimney, blazing with drift-wood, gave light and heat to the apartment, and brought into flickering relief the boarded walls hung with the spoils of sea and shore, and glittering with gun-barrels. Fowling-pieces of all sizes, from the long ducking-gun mounted on a swivel for boat use to the light single-barrel or carbine, stood in racks against the walls; game-bags, revolvers in their holsters, hunting and fishing knives in their sheaths, depended from hooks above them. In one corner stood a harpoon; in another, two or three Indian spears for salmon. The carpetless floor and rude chairs and settles were covered with otter, mink, beaver, and a quantity of valuable seal-skins, with a few larger pelts of the bear and elk.

The only attempt at decoration was the displayed wings and breasts of the wood and harlequin duck, the muir, the cormorant, the gull, the gannet, and the femininely delicate half-mourning of petrel and plover, nailed against the wall. The influence of the sea was dominant above all, and asserted its saline odors even through the spice of the curling drift-wood smoke that half veiled the ceiling.

A berry-eyed old Indian woman with the complexion of dried salmon; her daughter, also with berry eyes, and with a face that seemed wholly made of a moist laugh; 'Yellow Bob,' a Digger 'buck,' so called from the prevailing ochre markings of his cheek, and 'Washooh,' an ex-chief; a nondescript in a blanket, looking like a cheap and dirty doll whose fibrous hair was badly nailed on his carved wooden head, composed the Culpepper household. While the two former were preparing supper in the adjacent dining-room, Yellow Bob, relieved of his burden of game, appeared on the gallery and beckoned mysteriously to his master through the window. James Culpepper went out, returned quickly, and after a minute's hesitation and an uneasy glance towards his sister,

who had meantime pushed back her sou'-
wester from her forehead, and without taking
off her jacket had dropped into a chair before the fire with her back towards him, took
his gun noiselessly from the rack, and saying
carelessly that he would be back in a moment, disappeared.

Left to herself, Maggie coolly pulled off
her long boots and stockings, and comfortably opposed to the fire two very pretty
feet and ankles, whose delicate purity was
slightly blue-bleached by confinement in the
tepid sea - water. The contrast of their
waxen whiteness with her blue woolen skirt,
and with even the skin of her sunburnt
hands and wrists, apparently amused her,
and she sat for some moments with her
elbows on her knees, her skirts slightly
raised, contemplating them, and curling her
toes with evident satisfaction. The firelight
playing upon the rich coloring of her face,
the fringe of jet-black curls that almost met
the thick sweep of eyebrows, and left her
only a white strip of forehead, her short
upper lip and small chin, rounded but reso-
lute, completed a piquant and striking figure.
The rich brown shadows on the smoke-stained
walls and ceiling, the occasional starting into

relief of the scutcheons of brilliant plumage, and the momentary glitter of the steel barrels, made a quaint background to this charming picture. Sitting there, and following some lingering memory of her tramp on the Marsh, she hummed to herself a few notes of the bugle call that had impressed her — at first softly, and finally with the full pitch of her voice.

Suddenly she stopped.

There was a faint and unmistakable rapping on the floor beneath her. It was distinct, but cautiously given, as if intended to be audible to her alone. For a moment she stood upright, her feet still bare and glistening, on the otter skin that served as a rug. There were two doors to the room, one from which her brother had disappeared, which led to the steps, the other giving on the back gallery, looking inland. With a quick instinct she caught up her gun and ran to that one, but not before a rapid scramble near the railing was followed by a cautious opening of the door. She was just in time to shut it on the extended arm and light blue sleeve of an army overcoat that protruded through the opening, and for a moment threw her whole weight against it.

" A dhrop of whiskey, Miss, for the love of God."

She retained her hold, cocked her weapon, and stepped back a pace from the door. The blue sleeve was followed by the rest of the overcoat, and a blue cap with the infantry blazoning, and the letter H on its peak. They were for the moment more distinguishable than the man beneath them — grimed and blackened with the slime of the Marsh. But what could be seen of his mud-stained face was more grotesque than terrifying. A combination of weakness and audacity, insinuation and timidity struggled through the dirt for expression. His small blue eyes were not ill-natured, and even the intruding arm trembled more from exhaustion than passion.

" On'y a dhrop, Miss," he repeated piteously, "and av ye pleeze, quick! afore I'm stharved with the cold entoirely."

She looked at him intently — without lowering her gun.

" Who are you ? "

" Thin, it's the truth I'll tell ye, Miss — whisth then ! " he said in a half-whisper ; " I'm a desarter ! "

" Then it was *you* that was doggin' us on the Marsh ? "

" It was the sarjint I was lavin', Miss."

She looked at him hesitatingly.

"Stay outside there; if you move a step into the room, I 'll blow you out of it."

He stepped back on the gallery. She closed the door, bolted it, and still holding the gun, opened a cupboard, poured out a glass of whiskey, and returning to the door, opened it and handed him the liquor.

She watched him drain it eagerly, saw the fiery stimulant put life into his shivering frame, trembling hands, and kindle his dull eye — and — quietly raised her gun again.

" Ah, put it down, Miss, put it down! Fwhot 's the use? Sure the bullets yee carry in them oiyes of yours is more deadly! It 's out here oi 'll sthand, glory be to God, all night, without movin' a fut till the sarjint comes to take me, av ye won't levil them oiyes at me like that. Ah, whirra! look at that now! but it's a gooddess she is — the livin' Jaynus of warr, standin' there like a statoo, wid her alybaster fut put forward."

In her pride and conscious superiority, any suggestion of shame at thus appearing before a common man and a mendicant was as impossible to her nature as it would have been to a queen or the goddess of his simile.

His presence and his compliment alike passed her calm modesty unchallenged. The wretched scamp recognized the fact and felt its power, and it was with a superstitious reverence asserting itself through his native extravagance that he raised his grimy hand to his cap in military salute and became respectfully rigid.

"Then the sodgers were huntin' *you?*" she said thoughtfully, lowering her weapon.

"Thrue for you, Miss — they worr, and it's meself that was lyin' flat in the ditch wid me faytures makin' an illigant cast in the mud — more betoken, as ye see even now — and the sarjint and his daytail thrampin' round me. It was thin that the mortial cold sthruck thro' me mouth, and made me wake for the whiskey that would resthore me."

"What did you desert fer?"

"Ah, list to that now! Fwhat did I desart fer? Shure ev there was the ghost of an inemy round, it's meself that would be in the front now! But it was the letthers from me ould mother, Miss, that is sthruck wid a mortial illness — long life to her! — in County Clare, and me sisthers in Ninth Avenue in New York, fornint the daypo, that is brekken their harruts over me listin' in

the Fourth Infanthry to do duty in a haythen wilderness. Av it was the cavalry —
and it's me own father that was in the In-
nishkillen Dthragoons, Miss — oi would n't
moind. Wid a horse betune me legs, it's
on parade oi'd be now, Miss, and not wan-
dhering over the bare flure of the Marsh,
stharved wid the cold, the thirst, and hun-
ger, wid the mud and the moire thick on me ;
facin' an illigant young leddy as is the ekal
ov a Fayld Marshal's darter — not to sphake
ov Kernal Preston's — ez could n't hold a
candle to her."

Brought up on the Spanish frontier, Maggie Culpepper was one of the few American
girls who was not familiar with the Irish
race. The rare smile that momentarily lit
up her petulant mouth seemed to justify the
intruder's praise. But it passed quickly,
and she returned dryly :

" That means you want more drink, suthin'
to eat, and clothes. Suppose my brother
comes back and ketches you here ? "

" Shure, Miss, he's just now hunten me,
along wid his two haythen Diggers, beyond
the laygoon there. It worr the yellar one
that sphotted me lyin' there in the ditch ;
it worr only your own oiyes, Miss — more

power to their beauty for that! — that saw
me folly him unbeknownst here; and that
desaved them, ye see!"

The young girl remained for an instant
silent and thoughtful.

"We're no friends of the Fort," she said
finally, "but I don't reckon for that reason
my brother will cotton to *you*. Stay out
thar where ye are, till I come to ye. If you
hear me singin' again, you'll know he's
come back, and ye'd better scoot with what
you've already got, and be thankful."

She shut the door again and locked it,
went into the dining-room, returned with
some provisions wrapped in paper, took a
common wicker flask from the wall, passed
into her brother's bedroom, and came out
with a flannel shirt, overalls, and a coarse
Indian blanket, and, reopening the door,
placed them before the astonished and delighted vagabond. His eye glistened; he
began, "Glory be to God," but for once his
habitual extravagance failed him. Nature
triumphed with a more eloquent silence over
his well-worn art. He hurriedly wiped his
begrimed face and eyes with the shirt she
had given him, and catching the sleeve of
her rough pea-jacket in his dirty hand,
raised it to his lips.

" Go ! " she said imperiously. " Get away while you can."

" Av it vas me last words — it 's speechless oi am," he stammered, and disappeared over the railing.

She remained for a moment holding the door half open, and gazing into the darkness that seemed to flow in like a tide. Then she shut it, and going into her bedroom resumed her interrupted toilette. When she emerged again she was smartly stockinged and slippered, and even the blue serge skirt was exchanged for a bright print, with a white fichu tied around her throat. An attempt to subdue her rebellious curls had resulted in the construction from their ruins of a low Norman arch across her forehead with pillared abutments of ringlets. When her brother returned a few moments later she did not look up, but remained, perhaps a little ostentatiously, bending over the fire.

" Bob allowed that the Fort boat was huntin' *men* — deserters, I reckon," said Jim aggrievedly. " Wanted me to believe that he *saw* one on the Marsh hidin'. On'y an Injin lie, I reckon, to git a little extra fire-water, for toting me out to the bresh on a fool's errand."

" Oh, *that's* where you went ! " said Maggie, addressing the fire. " Since when hev you tuk partnership with the Guv'nment and Kernel Preston to hunt up and take keer of their property ? "

" Well, I ain't goin' to hev such wreckage as they pick up and enlist set adrift on our marshes, Mag," said Jim decidedly.

" What would you hev done had you ketched him ? " said Maggie, looking suddenly into her brother's face.

" Given him a dose of snipe-shot that he'd remember, and be thankful it was n't slugs," said Jim promptly. Observing a deeper seriousness in her attitude, he added, " Why, if it was in war-time he'd get a *ball* from them sodgers on sight."

" Yes ; but *you* ain't got no call to interfere," said Maggie.

" Ain't I ? Why, he's no better than an outlaw. I ain't sure that he has n't been stealin' or killin' somebody over theer."

" Not *that* man ! " said Maggie impulsively.

" Not what man ? " said her brother, facing her quickly.

" Why," returned Maggie, repairing her indiscretion with feminine dexterity, " not *any* man who might have knocked you and me over on the marshes in the dusk, and grabbed our guns."

" Wish he 'd hev tried it," said the brother, with a superior smile, but a quickly rising color. " Where d' ye suppose *I 'd* hev been all the while ? "

Maggie saw her mistake, and for the first time in her life resolved to keep a secret from her brother — overnight. " Supper 's gettin' cold," she said, rising.

They went into the dining-room — an apartment as plainly furnished as the one they had quitted, but in its shelves, cupboards, and closely fitting boarding bearing out the general nautical suggestion of the house — and seated themselves before a small table on which their frugal meal was spread. In this *tête-à-tête* position Jim suddenly laid down his knife and fork and stared at his sister.

" Hello ! "

" What 's the matter ? " said Maggie, starting slightly. " How you do skeer one."

" Who 's been prinkin', eh ? "

" My ha'r was in kinks all along o' that hat," said Maggie, with a return of higher color, " and I had to straighten it. It's a boy's hat, not a girl's."

" But that necktie and that gown — and all those frills and tuckers ? " continued Jim generalizing, with a rapid twirling of his fingers over her. " Are you expectin' Judge Martin, or the Expressman, this evening ? "

Judge Martin was the lawyer of Logport, who had proven her father's will, and had since raved about his single interview with the Kingfisher's beautiful daughter ; the Expressman was a young fellow who was popularly supposed to have left his heart while delivering another valuable package on Maggie in person, and had "never been the same man since." It was a well-worn fraternal pleasantry that had done duty many a winter's evening, as a happy combination of moral admonition and cheerfulness. Maggie usually paid it the tribute of a quick little laugh and a sisterly pinch, but that evening those marks of approbation were withheld.

" Jim dear," said she, when their Spartan repast was concluded and they were reëstablished before the living-room fire. " What was it the Redwood Mill Kempany offered you for that piece near Dead Man's Slough ? "

Jim took his pipe from his lips long enough to say, " Ten thousand dollars," and put it back again.

" And what do ye kalkilate all our property, letting alone this yer house, and the driftwood front, is worth all together? "

" Includin' wot the Gov'nment owes us ? — for that 's all ours, ye know? " said Jim quickly.

" No — leavin' that out — jest for greens, you know," suggested Maggie.

" Well nigh onter a hundred and seventy-five thousand dollars, I reckon, by and large."   *

" That 's a heap o' money, Jim! I reckon old Kernel Preston would n't raise that in a hundred years," continued Maggie, warming her knees by the fire.

" In five million years," said Jim, promptly sweeping away further discussion. After a pause he added, " You and me, Mag, kin see anybody's pile, and go 'em fifty thousand better."

There were a few moments of complete silence, in which Maggie smoothed her knees, and Jim's pipe, which seemed to have become gorged and apoplectic with its owner's wealth, snored unctuously.

"Jim dear, what if — it's on'y an idea of mine, you know — what if you sold that piece to the Redwood Mill, and we jest tuk that money and — and — and jest lifted the ha'r offer them folks at Logport? Jest astonished 'em! Jest tuk the best rooms in that new hotel, got a hoss and buggy, dressed ourselves, you and me, fit to kill, and made them Fort people take a back seat in the Lord's Tabernacle, oncet for all. You see what I mean, Jim," she said hastily, as her brother seemed to be succumbing, like his pipe, in apoplectic astonishment, "jest on'y to *show* 'em what we *could* do if we keerd. Lord! when we done it and spent the money we'd jest snap our fingers and skip back yer ez nat'ral ez life! Ye don't think, Jim," she said, suddenly turning half fiercely upon him, "that I'd allow to *live* among 'em — to stay a menet after that!"

Jim laid down his pipe and gazed at his sister with stony deliberation. "And — what — do — you — kalkilate — to make by all that?" he said with scornful distinctness.

"Why, jest to show 'em we *have* got money, and could buy 'em all up if we

wanted to," returned Maggie, sticking boldly
to her guns, albeit with a vague conviction
that her fire was weakened through eleva-
tion, and somewhat alarmed at the deliberation of the enemy.

"And you mean to say they don't know
it now," he continued with slow derision.

"No," said Maggie. "Why, theer's that
new school-marm over at Logport, you know,
Jim, the one that wanted to take your picter
in your boat for a young smuggler or fancy
pirate or Eyetalian fisherman, and allowed
that you'r handsomed some, and offered to
pay you for sittin' — do you reckon *she'd*
believe you owned the land her schoolhouse
was built on. No! Lots of 'em don't. Lots
of 'em thinks we're poor and low down —
and them ez does n't, thinks " —

"What?" asked her brother sharply.

"That we're *mean*."

The quick color came to Jim's cheek.
"So," he said, facing her quickly, "for the
sake of a lot of riff-raff and scum that's
drifted here around us — jest for the sake of
cuttin' a swell before them — you'll go out
among the hounds ez allowed your mother
was a Spanish nigger or a kanaka, ez called
your father a pirate and landgrabber, ez

much as allowed he was shot by some one or killed himself a purpose, ez said you was a heathen and a looney because you did n't go to school or church along with their trash, ez kept away from Maw's sickness ez if it was smallpox, and Dad's fun'ral ez if he was a hoss-thief, and left you and me to watch his coffin on the marshes all night till the tide kem back. And now you — *you* that jined hands with me that night over our father lyin' there cold and despised — ez if he was a dead dog thrown up by the tide — and swore that ez long ez that tide ebbed and flowed it could n't bring you to them, or them to you agin! You now want — what? What? Why, to go and cast your lot among 'em, and live among 'em, and join in their God-forsaken holler foolishness, and — and — and " —

"Stop! It's a lie! I *did n't* say that. Don't you dare to say it!" said the girl, springing to her feet, and facing her brother in turn, with flashing eyes.

For a moment the two stared at each other — it might have been as in a mirror, so perfectly were their passions reflected in each line, shade, and color of the other's face. It was as if they had each confronted their own

passionate and willful souls, and were frightened. It had often occurred before, always
with the same invariable ending. The
young man's eyes lowered first; the girl's
filled with tears.

"Well, ef ye did n't mean that, what did
ye mean?" said Jim, sinking, with sullen
apology, back into his chair.

"I — only — meant it — for — for — revenge!" sobbed Maggie.

"Oh!" said Jim, as if allowing his higher
nature to be touched by this noble instinct.
"But I did n't jest see where the revenge
kem in."

"No? But, never mind now, Jim," said
Maggie, ostentatiously ignoring, after the
fashion of her sex, the trouble she had pro-
voked; "but to think — that — that — you
thought" — (sobbing).

"But I did n't, Mag" — (caressingly).

With this very vague and impotent conclusion, Maggie permitted herself to be
drawn beside her brother, and for a few moments they plumed each other's ruffled feathers, and smoothed each other's lifted crests,
like two beautiful young specimens of that
halcyon genus to which they were popularly
supposed to belong. At the end of half an

hour Jim rose, and, yawning slightly, said in a perfunctory way :

" Where 's the book ? "

The book in question was the Bible. It had been the self-imposed custom of these two young people to read aloud a chapter every night as their one vague formula of literary and religious discipline. When it was produced, Maggie, presuming on his affectionate and penitential condition, suggested that to-night he should pick out "suthin' interestin'." But this unorthodox frivolity was sternly put aside by Jim — albeit, by way of compromise, he agreed to " chance it," *i. e.*, open its pages at random.

He did so. Generally he allowed himself a moment's judicious pause for a certain chaste preliminary inspection necessary before reading aloud to a girl. To-night he omitted that modest precaution, and in a pleasant voice, which in reading was singularly free from colloquial infelicities of pronunciation, began at once :

" ' Curse ye Meroz, said the angel of the Lord, curse ye bitterly the inhabitants thereof ; because they came not to the help of the Lord, to the help of the Lord against the mighty.' "

"Oh, you looked first," said Maggie.

"I didn't now — honest Injin! I just opened."

"Go on," said Maggie, eagerly shoving him and interposing her neck over his shoulder.

And Jim continued Deborah's wonderful song of Jael and Sisera to the bitter end of its strong monosyllabic climax.

"There," he said, closing the volume, "that's what *I* call revenge. That's the real Scripture thing — no fancy frills theer."

"Yes; but, Jim dear, don't you see that she treated him first — sorter got round him with free milk and butter, and reg'larly blandished him," argued Maggie earnestly.

But Jim declined to accept this feminine suggestion, or to pursue the subject further, and after a fraternal embrace they separated for the night. Jim lingered long enough to look after the fastening of the door and windows, and Maggie remained for some moments at her casement, looking across the gallery to the Marsh beyond.

The moon had risen, the tide was half up. Whatever sign or trace of alien footprint or occupation had been there was already smoothly obliterated; even the configuration of the land had changed. A black cape had disappeared, a level line of shore had been eaten into by teeth of glistening silver. The whole dark surface of the Marsh was beginning to be streaked with shining veins as if a new life was coursing through it. Part of the open bay before the Fort, encroaching upon the shore, seemed in the moonlight to be reaching a white and outstretched arm towards the nest of the Kingfisher.

III.

THE reveille at Fort Redwood had been supplemented full five minutes by the voice of Lieutenant George Calvert's servant, before that young officer struggled from his bed. His head was splitting, his tongue and lips were dry and feverish, his bloodshot eyes were shrinking from the insufferable light of the day, his mind a confused medley of the past night and the present morning, of cards and wild revelry, and the vision of a reproachfully trim orderly standing at his door with reports and orders which he now held composedly in his hand. For Lieutenant Calvert had been enjoying a symposium variously known as " Stag Feed " and " A Wild Stormy Night " with several of his brother officers, and a sickening conviction that it was not the first or the last time he had indulged in these festivities. At that moment he loathed himself, and then after the usual derelict fashion cursed the fate that had sent him, after graduating, to a frontier garrison — the dull monotony of whose duties made the Border horse-play of dissipation a relief. Already he had reached the miserable point of envying the veteran capacities of his superiors and equals. " If I could drink like Kirby or Crowninshield, or if there was any other cursed thing a man could do in this hole," he had wretchedly repeated to himself, after each misspent occasion, and yet already he was looking forward to them as part of a ' sub's ' duty and worthy his emulation. Already the dream of social recreation fostered by West Point had been rudely dispelled. Beyond the garrison circle of Colonel Preston's family and two officers' wives, there was no society. The vague distrust and civil jealousy with which some frontier communities regard the Federal power, heightened in this instance by the uncompromising attitude the Government had taken towards the settlers' severe Indian policy, had kept the people of Logport aloof from the Fort. The regimental band might pipe to them on Saturdays, but they would not dance.

Howbeit, Lieutenant Calvert dressed himself with uncertain hands but mechanical regularity and neatness, and, under the automatic training of discipline and duty, managed to button his tunic tightly over his feelings, to pull himself together with his sword-belt, compressing a still cadet-like waist, and to present that indescribable combination of precision and jauntiness which his brother officers too often allowed to lapse into frontier carelessness. His closely clipped light hair, yet dripping from a plunge in the cold water, had been brushed and parted with military exactitude, and when surmounted by his cap, with the peak in an artful suggestion of extra smartness tipped forward over his eyes, only his pale face — a shade lighter than his little blonde moustache — showed his last night's excesses. He was mechanically reaching for his sword and staring confusedly at the papers on his table when his servant interrupted :

"Major Bromley arranged that Lieuten-

ant Kirby takes your sash this morning, as
you 're not well, sir; and you 're to report for
special to the colonel," he added, pointing
discreetly to the envelope.

Touched by this consideration of his superior, Major Bromley, who had been one of
the veterans of last night's engagement, Calvert mastered the contents of the envelope
without the customary anathema of specials,
said, "Thank you, Parks," and passed out
on the veranda.

The glare of the quiet sunlit quadrangle,
clean as a well-swept floor, the whitewashed
walls and galleries of the barrack buildings
beyond, the white and green palisade of
officers' cottages on either side, and the glitter of a sentry's bayonet, were for a moment
intolerable to him. Yet, by a kind of subtle
irony, never before had the genius and spirit
of the vocation he had chosen seemed to be
as incarnate as in the scene before him. Seclusion, self-restraint, cleanliness, regularity,
sobriety, the atmosphere of a wholesome life,
the austere reserve of a monastery without
its mysterious or pensive meditation, were all
there. To escape which, he had of his own
free will successively accepted a fool's distraction, the inevitable result of which was,

the viewing of them the next morning with
tremulous nerves and aching eyeballs.

An hour later, Lieutenant George Calvert
had received his final instructions from Colonel Preston to take charge of a small detachment to recover and bring back certain
deserters, but notably one, Dennis M'Caffrey of Company H, charged additionally
with mutinous solicitation and example. As
Calvert stood before his superior, that distinguished officer, whose oratorical powers had
been considerably stimulated through a long
course of " returning thanks for the Army,"
slightly expanded his chest and said pater-
nally :

" I am aware, Mr. Calvert, that duties
of this kind are somewhat distasteful to
young officers, and are apt to be considered
in the light of police detail; but I must re-
mind you that no one part of a soldier's
duty can be held more important or honorable than another, and that the fulfilment of
any one, however trifling, must, with honor
to himself and security to his comrades, receive his fullest devotion. A sergeant and a
file of men might perform your duty, but I
require, in addition, the discretion, courtesy,
and consideration of a gentleman who will

command an equal respect from those with
whom his duty brings him in contact. The
unhappy prejudices which the settlers show
to the military authority here render this, as
you are aware, a difficult service, but I believe that you will, without forgetting the
respect due to yourself and the Government
you represent, avoid arousing these prejudices by any harshness, or inviting any con-
flict with the civil authority. The limits of
their authority you will find in your written
instructions; but you might gain their confidence, and impress them, Mr. Calvert, with
the idea of your being their *auxiliary* in the
interests of justice — you understand. Even
if you are unsuccessful in bringing back the
men, you will do your best to ascertain if
their escape has been due to the sympathy
of the settlers, or even with their preliminary
connivance. They may not be aware that
inciting enlisted men to desert is a criminal
offence ; you will use your own discretion in
informing them of the fact or not, as occasion may serve you. I have only to add,
that while you are on the waters of this bay
and the land covered by its tides, you have
no opposition of authority, and are responsible to no one but your military superiors.

Good-bye, Mr. Calvert. Let me hear a good account of you."

Considerably moved by Colonel Preston's manner, which was as paternal and real as his rhetoric was somewhat perfunctory, Calvert half forgot his woes as he stepped from the commandant's piazza. But he had to face a group of his brother officers, who were awaiting him.

"Good-bye, Calvert," said Major Bromley; "a day or two out on grass won't hurt you — and a change from commissary whiskey will put you all right. By the way, if you hear of any better stuff at Westport than they're giving us here, sample it and let us know. Take care of yourself. Give your men a chance to talk to you now and then, and you may get something from them, especially Donovan. Keep your eye on Ramon. You can trust your sergeant straight along."

"Good-bye, George," said Kirby. "I suppose the old man told you that, although no part of a soldier's duty was better than another, your service was a very delicate one, just fitted for you, eh? He always does when he's cut out some hellish scrub-work for a chap. And told you, too, that as long

as you did n't go ashore, and kept to a dis-
patch-boat, or an eight-oared gig, where you
could n't deploy your men, or dress a line,
you 'd be invincible."

" He did say something like that," smiled
Calvert, with an uneasy recollection, however, that it was *the* part of his superior's
speech that particularly impressed him.

" Of course," said Kirby gravely, " *that*,
as an infantry officer, is clearly your duty."

" And don't forget, George," said Rollins
still more gravely, " that, whatever may be-
fall you, you belong to a section of that
numerically small but powerfully diversified
organization — the American Army. Remember that in the hour of peril you can ad-
dress your men in any language, and be perfectly understood. And remember that when
you proudly stand before them, the eyes not
only of your own country, but of nearly all
the others, are upon you! Good-bye, Geor-
gey. I heard the major hint something
about whiskey. They say that old pirate,
Kingfisher Culpepper, had a stock of the real
thing from Robertson County laid in his
shebang on the Marsh just before he died.
Pity we are n't on terms with them, for the
cubs cannot drink it, and might be induced

to sell. Should n't wonder, by the way, if your friend M'Caffrey was hanging round somewhere there; he always had a keen scent. You might confiscate it as an "incitement to desertion," you know. The girl's pretty, and ought to be growing up now."

But haply at this point the sergeant stopped further raillery by reporting the detachment ready; and drawing his sword, Calvert, with a confused head, a remorseful heart, but an unfaltering step, marched off his men on his delicate mission.

It was four o'clock when he entered Jonesville. Following a matter-of-fact idea of his own, he had brought his men the greater distance by a circuitous route through the woods, thus avoiding the ostentatious exposure of his party on the open bay in a well-manned boat to an extended view from the three leagues of shore and marsh opposite. Crossing the stream, which here separated him from the Dedlow Marsh by the common ferry, he had thus been enabled to halt unperceived below the settlement and occupy the two roads by which the fugitives could escape inland. He had deemed it not impossible that, after the previous visit of the sergeant, the deserters hidden in the vicinity might return to Jonesville in the belief that the visit would not be repeated so soon. Leaving a part of his small force to patrol the road and another to deploy over the upland meadows, he entered the village. By the exercise of some boyish diplomacy and a certain prepossessing grace, which he knew when and how to employ, he became satisfied that the objects of his quest were not *there* — however, their whereabouts might have been known to the people. Dividing his party again, he concluded to take a corporal and a few men and explore the lower marshes himself.

The preoccupation of duty, exercise, and perhaps, above all, the keen stimulus of the iodine-laden salt air seemed to clear his mind and invigorate his body. He had never been in the Marsh before, and enjoyed its novelty with the zest of youth. It was the hour when the tide of its feathered life was at its flood. Clouds of duck and teal passing from the fresh water of the river to the salt pools of the marshes perpetually swept his path with flying shadows; at times it seemed as if even the uncertain ground around him itself arose and sped away on dusky wings. The vicinity of hidden pools and sloughs was betrayed by startled splashings; a few paces from their marching feet arose the sunlit pinions of a swan. The air was filled with multitudinous small cries and pipings. In this vocal confusion it was some minutes before he recognized the voice of one of his out-flankers calling to the other.

An important discovery had been made. In a long tongue of bushes that ran down to the Marsh they had found a mud-stained uniform, complete even to the cap, bearing the initial of the deserter's company.

"Is there any hut or cabin hereabouts, Schmidt?" asked Calvert.

"Dot vos schoost it, Lefdennun," replied his corporal. "Dot vos de shanty from der Kingvisher — old Gulbebber. I pet a dollar, py shimminy, dot der men haf der gekommt."

He pointed through the brake to a long, low building that now raised itself, white in the sunlight, above the many blackened piles. Calvert saw in a single reconnoitring glance that it had but one approach — the flight of steps from the Marsh. Instructing his men to fall in on the outer edge of the brake and await his orders, he quickly made his way across the space and ascended the steps. Passing along the gallery he knocked at the front door. There was no response. He repeated his knock. Then the window beside it opened suddenly, and he was confronted with the double-muzzle of a long ducking-gun. Glancing instinctively along the barrels, he saw at their other extremity the bright eyes, brilliant color, and small set mouth of a remarkably handsome girl. It was the fact, and to the credit of his training, that he paid more attention to the eyes than to the challenge of the shining tubes before him.

"Jest stop where you are — will you!" said the girl determinedly.

Calvert's face betrayed not the slightest terror or surprise. Immovable as on parade, he carried his white gloved hand tð his cap, and said gently, "With pleasure."

"Oh yes," said the girl quickly; "but if you move a step I'll jest blow you and your gloves offer that railin' inter the Marsh."

"I trust not," returned Calvert, smiling.

"And why?"

"Because it would deprive me of the pleasure of a few moments' conversation with you — and I've only one pair of gloves with me."

He was still watching her beautiful eyes — respectfully, admiringly, and strategically. For he was quite convinced that if he *did* move she would certainly discharge one or both barrels at him.

"Where's the rest of you?" she continued sharply.

"About three hundred yards away, in the covert, not near enough to trouble you."

"Will they come here?"

"I trust not."

"You trust not?" she repeated scornfully. "Why?"

"Because they would be disobeying orders."

She lowered her gun slightly, but kept her black brows levelled at him. "I reckon I'm a match for *you*," she said, with a slightly contemptuous glance at his slight figure, and opened the door. For a moment they stood looking at each other. He saw, besides the handsome face and eyes that had charmed him, a tall slim figure, made broader across the shoulders by an open pea-jacket that showed a man's red flannel shirt belted at the waist over a blue skirt, with

the collar knotted by a sailor's black handkerchief, and turned back over a pretty
though sunburnt throat. She saw a rather
undersized young fellow in a jaunty undress
uniform, scant of gold braid, and bearing
only the single gold shoulder-bars of his
rank, but scrupulously neat and well fitting.
Light-colored hair cropped close, the small-
est of light moustaches, clear and penetrating blue eyes, and a few freckles completed
a picture that did not prepossess her. She
was therefore the more inclined to resent the
perfect ease and self-possession with which
the stranger carried off these manifest de-
fects before her.

She laid aside the gun, put her hands
deep in the pockets of her pea-jacket, and,
slightly squaring her shoulders, said curtly,
" What do you want ? "

" A very little information, which I trust
it will not trouble you to give me. My men
have just discovered the uniform belonging
to a deserter from the Fort lying in the
bushes yonder. Can you give me the slightest idea how it came there ? "

" What right have you trapseing over our
property ? " she said, turning upon him
sharply, with a slight paling of color.

" None whatever."

" Then what did you come for ? "

" To ask that permission, in case you would give me no information."

" Why don't you ask my brother, and not a woman ? Were you afraid ? "

" He could hardly have done me the honor of placing me in more peril than you have," returned Calvert, smiling. " Then I have the pleasure of addressing Miss Culpepper ?"

" I 'm Jim Culpepper's sister."

" And, I believe, equally able to give or refuse the permission I ask."

" And what if I refuse ? "

" Then I have only to ask pardon for having troubled you, go back, and return here with the tide. You don't resist *that* with a shot-gun, do you ? " he asked pleasantly.

Maggie Culpepper was already familiar with the accepted theory of the supreme jurisdiction of the Federal Sea. She half turned her back upon him, partly to show her contempt, but partly to evade the domination of his clear, good-humored, and self-sustained little eyes.

" I don't know anythin' about your deserters, nor what rags o' theirs happen to be floated up here," she said, angrily, "and don't care to. You kin do what you like."

"Then I'm afraid I should remain here a little longer, Miss Culpepper; but my duty " —

"Your wot?" she interrupted, disdainfully.

"I suppose I *am* talking shop," he said smilingly. "Then my business" —

"Your business — pickin' up half-starved runaways!"

"And, I trust, sometimes a kind friend," he suggested, with a grave bow.

"You *trust?* Look yer, young man," she said, with her quick, fierce, little laugh, "I reckon you *trust* a heap too much!" She would like to have added, "with your freckled face, red hair, and little eyes" — but this would have obliged her to face them again, which she did not care to do.

Calvert stepped back, lifted his hand to his cap, still pleasantly, and then walked gravely along the gallery, down the steps, and towards the cover. From her window, unseen, she followed his neat little figure moving undeviatingly on, without looking to the left or right, and still less towards the house he had just quitted. Then she saw

the sunlight flash on cross-belt plates and
steel barrels, and a light blue line issued
from out the dark green bushes, round the
point, and disappeared. And then it suddenly occurred to her what she had been
doing! This, then, was her first step towards that fancy she had so lately conceived,
quarrelled over with her brother, and lay
awake last night to place anew, in spite of
all opposition! This was her brilliant idea
of dazzling and subduing Logport and the
Fort! Had she grown silly, or what had
happened? Could she have dreamed of the
coming of this whipper-snapper, with his insufferable airs, after that beggarly deserter?
I am afraid that for a few moments the
miserable fugitive had as small a place in
Maggie's sympathy as the redoubtable whipper-snapper himself. And now the cherished
dream of triumph and conquest was over!
What a "looney" she had been! Instead
of inviting him in, and outdoing him in
"company manners," and "fooling" him
about the deserter, and then blazing upon
him afterwards at Logport in the glory of
her first spent wealth and finery, she had
driven him away!

And now "he'll go and tell — tell the

Fort girls of his hairbreadth escape from the claws of the Kingfisher's daughter!"

The thought brought a few bitter tears to her eyes, but she wiped them away. The thought brought also the terrible conviction that Jim was right, that there could be nothing but open antagonism between them and the traducers of their parents, as she herself had instinctively shown! But she presently wiped that conviction away also, as she had her tears.

Half an hour later she was attracted by the appearance from the windows of certain straggling blue spots on the upland that seemed moving diagonally towards the Marsh. She did not know that it was Calvert's second "detail" joining him, but believed for a moment that he had not yet departed, and was strangely relieved. Still later the frequent disturbed cries of coot, heron, and marsh-hen, recognizing the presence of unusual invaders of their solitude, distracted her yet more, and forced her at last with increasing color and an uneasy sense of shyness to steal out to the gallery for a swift furtive survey of the Marsh. But an utterly unexpected sight met her eyes, and kept her motionless.

The birds were rising everywhere and drifting away with querulous perturbation before a small but augmented blue detachment that was moving with monotonous regularity towards the point of bushes where she had seen the young officer previously disappear. In their midst, between two soldiers with fixed bayonets, marched the man whom even at that distance she instantly recognized as the deserter of the preceding night, in the very clothes she had given him. To complete her consternation, a little to the right marched the young officer also, but accompanied by, and apparently on the most amicable terms with, Jim — her own brother!

To forget all else and dart down the steps, flying towards the point of bushes, scarcely knowing why or what she was doing, was to Maggie the impulse and work of a moment. When she had reached it the party were not twenty paces away. But here a shyness and hesitation again seized her, and she shrank back in the bushes with an instinctive cry to her brother inarticulate upon her lips. They came nearer, they were opposite to her; her brother Jim keeping step with the invader, and even conversing with him

with an animation she had seldom seen upon
his face — they passed ! She had been unnoticed except by one. The roving eye of the
deserter had detected her handsome face
among the leaves, slightly turned towards it,
and poured out his whole soul in a single
swift wink of eloquent but indescribable confidence.

When they had quite gone, she crept
back to the house, a little reassured, but still
tremulous. When her brother returned at
nightfall, he found her brooding over the
fire, in the same attitude as on the previous
night.

" I reckon ye might hev seen me go by
with the sodgers," he said, seating himself
beside her, a little awkwardly, and with an
unusual assumption of carelessness.

Maggie, without looking up, was languidly
surprised. He had been with the soldiers —
and where ?

" About two hours ago I met this yer
Leftenant Calvert," he went on with increasing awkwardness, " and — oh, I say, Mag —
he said he saw you, and hoped he had n't
troubled ye, and — and — ye saw him,
did n't ye ? "

Maggie, with all the red of the fire concentrated in her cheek as she gazed at the flame, believed carelessly " that she had seen a shrimp in uniform asking questions."

" Oh, he ain't a bit stuck up," said Jim quickly, " that's what I like about him. He's ez nat'ral ez you be, and tuck my arm, walkin' around, careless-like, laffen at what he was doin', ez ef it was a game, and he was n't sole commander of forty men. He's only a year or two older than me — and — and " — he stopped and looked uneasily at Maggie.

" So ye've bin craw-fishin' agin ? " said Maggie, in her deepest and most scornful contralto.

" Who's craw-fishin' ? " he retorted, angrily.

" What's this backen out o' what you said yesterday ?   What's all this trucklin' to the Fort now ? "

" What ? Well now, look yer," said Jim, rising suddenly, with reproachful indignation, " darned if I don't jest tell ye everythin'. I promised *him* I would n't. He allowed it would frighten ye."

" *Frighten me !* " repeated Maggie contemptuously, nevertheless with her cheek paling again. "Frighten me — with what ? "

"Well, since yer so cantankerous, look yer. We 've been robbed ! "

"Robbed ? " echoed Maggie, facing him.

"Yes, robbed by that same deserter. Robbed of a suit of my clothes, and my whiskey-flask, and the darned skunk had 'em on. And if it had n't bin for that Leftenant Calvert, and my givin' him permission to hunt him over the Marsh, we would n't have caught him."

"Robbed ? " repeated Maggie again, vaguely.

"Yes, robbed ! Last night, afore we came home. He must hev got in yer while we was comin' from the boat."

"Did, did that Leftenant say so ? " stammered Maggie.

"Say it, of course he did ! and so do I," continued Jim, impatiently. "Why, there were my very clothes on his back, and he dare n't deny it. And if you 'd hearkened to me jest now, instead of flyin' off in tantrums, you 'd see that *that* 's jest how we got him, and how me and the Leftenant joined hands in it. I did n't give him permission to hunt deserters, but *thieves*. I did n't help him to ketch the man that deserted from *him*, but the skunk that took *my* clothes. For when the Leftenant found the man's old uniform in the bush, he nat'rally kalkilated he must hev got some other duds near by in some underhand way. Don't you see? eh? Why, look, Mag. Darned if you ain't skeered after all! Who'd hev thought it? There now — sit down, dear. Why, you're white ez a gull."

He had his arm round her as she sank back in the chair again with a forced smile.

"There now," he said with fraternal superiority, "don't mind it, Mag, any more. Why, it's all over now. You bet he won't trouble us agin, for the Leftenant sez that now he's found out to be a thief, they'll jest turn him over to the police, and he's sure o' getten six months' state prison fer stealin' and burglarin' in our house. But" — he stopped suddenly and looked at his sister's contracted face; "look yer, Mag, you're sick, that's what's the matter. Take suthin'" —

"I'm better now," she said with an effort; "it's only a kind o' blind chill I must hev got on the Marsh last night. What's that?"

She had risen, and grasping her brother's arm tightly had turned quickly to the window. The casement had suddenly rattled.

" It's only the wind gettin' up. It looked like a sou'wester when I came in. Lot o' scud flyin'. But *you* take some quinine, Mag. Don't *you* go now and get down sick like Maw."

Perhaps it was this well-meant but infelicitous reference that brought a moisture to her dark eyes, and caused her lips to momentarily quiver. But it gave way to a quick determined setting of her whole face as she turned it once more to the fire, and said, slowly :

" I reckon I'll sleep it off, if I go to bed now. What time does the tide fall."

" About three, unless this yer wind piles it up on the Marsh afore then. Why ? "

" I was only wonderin' if the boat wus safe," said Maggie, rising.

" You'd better hoist yourself outside some quinine, instead o' talken about those things," said Jim, who preferred to discharge his fraternal responsibility by active medication. " You are n't fit to read tonight."

" Good night, Jim," she said suddenly, stopping before him.

" Good night, Mag." He kissed her with protecting and amiable toleration, generously referring her hot hands and feverish lips to that vague mystery of feminine complaint which man admits without indorsing.

They separated. Jim, under the stimulus of the late supposed robbery, ostentatiously fastening the doors and windows with assuring comments, calculated to inspire confidence in his sister's startled heart. Then he went to bed. He lay awake long enough to be pleasantly conscious that the wind had increased to a gale, and to be lulled again to sleep by the cosy security of the heavily timbered and tightly sealed dwelling that seemed to ride the storm like the ship it resembled. The gale swept through the piles beneath him and along the gallery as through bared spars and over wave-washed decks. The whole structure, attacked above, below, and on all sides by the fury of the wind, seemed at times to be lifted in the air. Once or twice the creaking timbers simulated the sound of opening doors and passing footsteps, and again dilated as if the gale had forced a passage through. But Jim slept on peacefully, and was at last only aroused by the brilliant sunshine staring through his window from the clear wind-swept blue arch beyond.

Dressing himself lazily, he passed into the sitting-room and proceeded to knock at his sister's door, as was his custom ; he was amazed to find it open and the room empty. Entering hurriedly, he saw that her bed was undisturbed, as if it had not been occupied, and was the more bewildered to see a note ostentatiously pinned upon the pillow, addressed in pencil, in a large school-hand, "To Jim."

Opening it impatiently, he was startled to read as follows : —

"Don't be angry, Jim dear — but it was all my fault — and I did n't tell you. I knew all about the deserter, and I gave him the clothes and things that they say he stole. It was while you was out that night, and he came and begged of me, and was mournful and hidjus to behold. I thought I was helping him, and getting our revenge on the Fort, all at the same time. Don't be mad, Jim dear, and do not be frighted fer me. I 'm going over thar to make it all right — to free *him* of stealing — to have *you* left out of it all — and take it all on myself. Don't you be a bit feared for me. I ain't skeert of the wind or of going. I 'll close reef everything, clear the creek, stretch across to Injen Island, hugg the Point, and bear up fer Logport. Dear Jim — don't get mad — but I could n't

bear this fooling of you nor *him* — and that man
being took for stealing any longer ! — Your lov-
ing sister,   MAGGIE."

With a confused mingling of shame, anger, and sudden fear he ran out on the gallery. The tide was well up, half the Marsh
had already vanished, and the little creek
where he had moored his skiff was now an
empty shining river. The water was everywhere — fringing the tussocks of salt grass
with concentric curves of spume and drift,
or tumultuously tossing its white-capped
waves over the spreading expanse of the
lower bay. The low thunder of breakers in
the farther estuary broke monotonously on
the ear. But his eye was fascinated by a
dull shifting streak on the horizon, that,
even as he gazed, shuddered, whitened along
its whole line, and then grew ghastly gray
again. It was the ocean bar.

IV.

" WELL, I must say," said Cicely Preston, emphasizing the usual feminine imperative for perfectly gratuitous statement, as
she pushed back her chair from the comman-

dant's breakfast table, " I *must* really say
that I don't see anything particularly heroic
in doing something wrong, lying about it
just to get other folks into trouble, and then
rushing off to do penance in a high wind and
an open boat. But she's pretty, and wears
a man's shirt and coat, and of course *that*
settles anything. But why earrings and wet
white stockings and slippers? And why
that Gothic arch of front and a boy's hat?
That's what I simply ask ; " and the youngest daughter of Colonel Preston rose from
the table, shook out the skirt of her pretty
morning dress, and, placing her little thumbs
in the belt of her smart waist, paused wither-
ingly for a reply.

" You are most unfair, my child," returned Colonel Preston gravely. " Her
giving food and clothes to a deserter may
have been only an ordinary instinct of humanity towards a fellow-creature who appeared to be suffering, to say nothing of
M'Caffrey's plausible tongue. But her periling her life to save him from an unjust
accusation, and her desire to shield her
brother's pride from ridicule, is altogether
praiseworthy and extraordinary. And the
moral influence of her kindness was strong

enough to make that scamp refuse to tell the plain truth that might implicate her in an indiscretion, though it saved him from state prison."

"He knew you would n't believe him if he had said the clothes were given to him," retorted Miss Cicely, "so I don't see where the moral influence comes in. As to her periling her life, those Marsh people are amphibious anyway, or would be in those clothes. And as to her motive, why, papa, I heard you say in this very room, and afterwards to Mr. Calvert, when you gave him instructions, that you believed those Culpeppers were capable of enticing away deserters; and you forget the fuss you had with her savage brother's lawyer about that water front, and how you said it was such people who kept up the irritation between the Civil and Federal power."

The colonel coughed hurriedly. It is the fate of all great organizers, military as well as civil, to occasionally suffer defeat in the family circle.

"The more reason," he said, soothingly, "why we should correct harsh judgments that spring from mere rumors. You should give yourself at least the chance of overcoming your prejudices, my child. Remember, too, that she is now the guest of the Fort."

" And she chooses to stay with Mrs. Bromley ! I 'm sure it 's quite enough for you and mamma to do duty — and Emily, who wants to know why Mr. Calvert raves so about her — without *my* going over there to stare."

Colonel Preston shook his head reproachfully, but eventually retired, leaving the field to the enemy. The enemy, a little pink in the cheeks, slightly tossed the delicate rings of its blonde crest, settled its skirts again at the piano, but after turning over the leaves of its music book, rose, and walked pettishly to the window.

But here a spectacle presented itself that for a moment dismissed all other thoughts from the girl's rebellious mind.

Not a dozen yards away, on the wind-swept parade, a handsome young fellow, apparently halted by the sentry, had impetuously turned upon him in an attitude of indignant and haughty surprise. To the quick fancy of the girl it seemed as if some disguised rustic god had been startled by the challenge of a mortal. Under an oilskin hat, like the *petasus*

of Hermes, pushed back from his white forehead, crisp black curls were knotted around
a head whose beardless face was perfect as
a cameo cutting. In the close-fitting blue
woolen jersey under his open jacket the
clear outlines and youthful grace of his upper
figure were revealed as clearly as in a
statue. Long fishing-boots reaching to his
thighs scarcely concealed the symmetry of
his lower limbs. Cricket and lawn-tennis,
knickerbockers and flannels had not at that
period familiarized the female eye to unfet-
tered masculine outline, and Cicely Preston,
accustomed to the artificial smartness and
regularity of uniform, was perhaps the more
impressed by the stranger's lawless grace.

The sentry had repeated his challenge ; an
angry flush was deepening on the intruder's
cheek. At this critical moment Cicely
threw open the French windows and stepped
upon the veranda.

The sentry saluted the familiar little
figure of his colonel's daughter with an ex-
planatory glance at the stranger. The young
fellow looked up — and the god became
human.

"I'm looking for my sister," he said, half
awkwardly, half defiantly ; "she's here,
somewhere."

" Yes — and perfectly safe, Mr. Culpepper, I think," said the arch-hypocrite with
dazzling sweetness ; " and we 're all so delighted. And so brave and plucky and
skillful in her to come all that way — and
for such a purpose."

" Then — you know — all about it " —
stammered Jim, more relieved than he had
imagined — " and that I " —

" That you were quite ignorant of your
sister helping the deserter. Oh yes, of
course," said Cicely, with bewildering
promptitude. " You see, Mr. Culpepper,
we girls are *so* foolish. I dare say *I* should
have done the same thing in her place, only
I should never have had the courage to do
what she did afterwards. You really must
forgive her. But won't you come in — *do*."
She stepped back, holding the window open
with the half-coaxing air of a spoiled child.
" This way is quickest. *Do* come." As he
still hesitated, glancing from her to the
house, she added, with a demure little laugh,
" Oh, I forget — this is Colonel Preston's
quarters, and I 'm his daughter."

And this dainty little fairy, so natural in
manner, so tasteful in attire, was one of the
artificial over-dressed creatures that his sister

had inveighed against so bitterly! Was Maggie really to be trusted? This new revelation coming so soon after the episode of the deserter staggered him. Nevertheless he hesitated, looking up with a certain boyish timidity into Cicely's dangerous eyes.

"Is — is — my sister there?"

"I'm expecting her with my mother every moment," responded this youthful but ingenious diplomatist sweetly; "she might be here now; but," she added with a sudden heart-broken flash of sympathy, "I know *how* anxious you both must be. *I'll* take you to her now. Only one moment, please." The opportunity of leading this handsome savage as it were in chains across the parade, before everybody, her father, her mother, her sister, and *his* — was not to be lost. She darted into the house, and reappeared with the daintiest imaginable straw hat on the side of her head, and demurely took her place at his side. "It's only over there, at Major Bromley's," she said, pointing to one of the vine-clad cottage quarters; but you are a stranger here, you know, and might get lost."

Alas! he was already that. For keeping

step with those fairy-like slippers, brushing
awkwardly against that fresh and pretty
skirt, and feeling the caress of the soft folds;
looking down upon the brim of that berib-
boned little hat, and more often meeting the
upturned blue eyes beneath it, Jim was suddenly struck with a terrible conviction of his
own contrasting coarseness and deficiencies.
How hideous those oiled canvas fishing-
trousers and pilot jacket looked beside this
perfectly fitted and delicately gowned girl!
He loathed his collar, his jersey, his turned-
back sou'wester, even his height, which
seemed to hulk beside her — everything, in
short, that the girl had recently admired.
By the time that they had reached Major
Bromley's door he had so far succumbed to
the fair enchantress and realized her ambition of a triumphant procession, that when
she ushered him into the presence of half a
dozen ladies and gentlemen he scarcely recognized his sister as the centre of attraction,
or knew that Miss Cicely's effusive greeting
of Maggie was her first one. "I knew he
was dying to see you after all you had *both*
passed through, and I brought him straight
here," said the diminutive Machiavelli, meeting the astonished gaze of her father and the

curious eyes of her sister with perfect calmness, while Maggie, full of gratitude and admiration of her handsome brother, forgot his momentary obliviousness, and returned her greeting warmly. Nevertheless, there was a slight movement of reserve among the gentlemen at the unlooked-for irruption of this sunburnt Adonis, until Calvert, disengaging himself from Maggie's side, came forward with his usual frank imperturbability and quiet tact, and claimed Jim as his friend and honored guest.

It then came out with that unostentatious simplicity which characterized the brother and sister, and was their secure claim to perfect equality with their entertainers, that Jim, on discovering his sister's absence, and fearing that she might be carried by the current towards the bar, had actually *swum the estuary* to Indian Island, and in an ordinary Indian canoe had braved the same tempestuous passage she had taken a few hours before. Cicely, listening to this recital with rapt attention, nevertheless managed to convey the impression of having fully expected it from the first. "Of course he'd have come here; if she'd only waited," she said, *sotto voce*, to her sister Emily.

"He's certainly the handsomer of the two," responded that young lady.

"Of course," returned Cicely, with a superior air, "don't you see she *copies* him."

Not that this private criticism prevented either from vying with the younger officers in their attentions to Maggie, with perhaps the addition of an open eulogy of her handsome brother, more or less invidious in comparison to the officers. "I suppose it's an active out-of-door life gives him that perfect grace and freedom," said Emily, with a slight sneer at the smartly belted Calvert. "Yes; and he don't drink or keep late hours," responded Cicely significantly. "His sister says they always retire before ten o'clock, and that although his father left him some valuable whiskey he seldom takes a drop of it." "Therein," gravely concluded Captain Kirby, "lies *our* salvation. If, after such a confession, Calvert does n't make the most of his acquaintance with young Culpepper to remove that whiskey from his path and bring it here, he's not the man I take him for."

Indeed, for the moment it seemed as if he was not. During the next three or four days, in which Colonel Preston had insisted

upon detaining his guests, Calvert touched
no liquor, evaded the evening poker parties
at quarters, and even prevailed upon some
of his brother officers to give them up for
the more general entertainment of the ladies.
Colonel Preston was politician enough to
avail himself of the popularity of Maggie's
adventure to invite some of the Logport people to assist him in honoring their neighbor.
Not only was the old feud between the Fort
and the people thus bridged over, but there
was no doubt that the discipline of the Fort
had been strengthened by Maggie's extravagant reputation as a mediator among the
disaffected rank and file. Whatever characteristic license the grateful Dennis M'Caffrey — let off with a nominal punishment —
may have taken in his praise of the " Quane
of the Marshes," it is certain that the men
worshiped her, and that the band patheti-
cally begged permission to serenade her the
last night of her stay.

At the end of that time, with a dozen
invitations, a dozen appointments, a dozen
vows of eternal friendship, much hand-shak-
ing, and accompanied by a number of the officers to their boat, Maggie and Jim departed.
They talked but little on their way home ;

by some tacit understanding they did not discuss those projects, only recalling certain scenes and incidents of their visit. By the time they had reached the little creek the silence and nervous apathy which usually follow excitement in the young seemed to have fallen upon them. It was not until after their quiet frugal supper that, seated beside the fire, Jim looked up somewhat self-consciously in his sister's grave and thoughtful face.

"Say, Mag, what was that idea o' yours about selling some land, and taking a house at Logport?"

Maggie looked up, and said passively, "Oh, *that* idea?"

"Yes."

"Why?"

"Well," said Jim somewhat awkwardly, "it *could* be done, you know. I'm willin'."

As she did not immediately reply, he continued uneasily, "Miss Preston says we kin get a nice little house that is near the Fort, until we want to build."

"Oh, then you *have* talked about it?"

"Yes — that is — why, what are ye thinkin' of, Mag? Was n't it *your* idea all along?" he said, suddenly facing her with querulous embarrassment. They had been sitting in their usual evening attitudes of Assyrian frieze profile, with even more than the usual Assyrian frieze similarity of feature.

"Yes; but, Jim dear, do you think it the best thing for — for us to do?" said Maggie, with half-frightened gravity.

At this sudden and startling exhibition of female inconsistency and inconsequence, Jim was for a moment speechless. Then he recovered himself, volubly, aggrievedly, and on his legs. What *did* she mean? Was he to give up understanding girls — or was it their sole vocation in life to impede masculine processes and shipwreck masculine conclusions? Here, after all she said the other night, after they had nearly "quo'lled" over her "set idees," after she'd "gone over all that foolishness about Jael and Sisera — and there wasn't any use for it — after she'd let him run on to them officers all he was goin' to do — nay, after *she* herself, for he had heard her, had talked to Calvert about it, she wanted to know *now* if it was best." He looked at the floor and the ceiling, as if expecting the tongued and grooved planks to cry out at this crowning enormity.

The cause of it had resumed her sad gaze

at the fire. Presently, without turning her head, she reached up her long, graceful arm, and clasping her brother's neck, brought his face down in profile with her own, cheek against cheek, until they looked like the double outlines of a medallion. Then she said — to the fire :

"Jim, do you think she 's pretty ? "

"Who ? " said Jim, albeit his color had already answered the question.

" You know *who*. Do you like her ? "

Jim here vaguely murmured to the fire that he thought her " kinder nice," and that she dressed mighty purty. "Ye know, Mag," he said with patronizing effusion, " you oughter get some gownds like hers."

" That would n't make me like her," said Maggie gravely.

" I don't know about that," said Jim politely, but with an appalling hopelessness of tone. After a pause he added slyly, " 'Pears to me *somebody else* thought somebody else mighty purty — eh ? "

To his discomfiture she did not solicit further information. After a pause he continued, still more archly :

" Do you like *him*, Mag ? "

" I think he 's a perfect gentleman," she said calmly.

He turned his eyes quickly from the glowing fire to her face. The cheek that had
been resting against his own was as cool as
the night wind that came through the open
door, and the whole face was as fixed and
tranquil as the upper stars.

V.

For a year the tide had ebbed and flowed
on the Dedlow Marsh unheeded before the
sealed and sightless windows of the "Kingfisher's Nest." Since the young birds had
flown to Logport, even the Indian caretakers
had abandoned the piled dwelling for their
old nomadic haunts in the "bresh." The
high spring tide had again made its annual
visit to the little cemetery of drift-wood, and,
as if recognizing another wreck in the deserted home, had hung a few memorial offerings on the blackened piles, softly laid a gar-
land of grayish drift before it, and then
sobbed itself out in the salt grass.

From time to time the faint echoes of the
Culpeppers' life at Logport reached the upland, and the few neighbors who had only
known them by hearsay shook their heads

over the extravagance they as yet only knew by report. But it was in the dead ebb of the tide and the waning daylight that the feathered tenants of the Marsh seemed to voice dismal prophecies of the ruin of their old master and mistress, and to give themselves up to gloomiest lamentation and querulous foreboding. Whether the traditional " bird of the air " had entrusted his secret to a few ornithological friends, or whether from a natural disposition to take gloomy views of life, it was certain that at this hour the vocal expression of the Marsh was hopeless and despairing. It was then that a dejected plover, addressing a mocking crew of sandpipers on a floating log, seemed to bewail the fortune that was being swallowed up by the riotous living and gambling debts of Jim. It was then that the querulous crane rose, and testily protested against the selling of his favorite haunt in the sandy peninsula, which only six months of Jim's excesses had made imperative. It was then that a mournful curlew, who, with the preface that he had always been really expecting it, reiterated the story that Jim had been seen more than once staggering home with nervous hands and sodden features from a debauch with the

younger officers ; it was the same desponding fowl who knew that Maggie's eyes had
more than once filled with tears at Jim's
failings, and had already grown more hollow
with many watchings. It was a flock of
wrangling teal that screamingly discussed
the small scandals, jealous heart-burnings,
and curious backbitings that had attended
Maggie's advent into society. It was the
high-flying brent who, knowing how the sensitive girl, made keenly conscious at every
turn of her defective training and ingenuous
ignorance, had often watched their evening
flight with longing gaze, now " honked "
dismally at the recollection. It was at this
hour and season that the usual vague lament-
ings of Dedlow Marsh seemed to find at last
a preordained expression. And it was at
such a time, when light and water were both
fading, and the blackness of the Marsh was
once more reasserting itself, that a small
boat was creeping along one of the tortuous
inlets, at times half hiding behind the bank
like a wounded bird. As it slowly pene-
trated inland it seemed to be impelled by its
solitary occupant in a hesitating uncertain
way, as if to escape observation rather than
as if directed to any positive bourn. Stop-

ping beside a bank of reeds at last, the
figure rose stoopingly, and drew a gun from
between its feet and the bottom of the boat.
As the light fell upon its face, it could be
seen that it was James Culpepper! James
Culpepper! hardly recognizable in the swollen features, bloodshot eyes, and tremulous
hands of that ruined figure! James Culpepper, only retaining a single trace of his former self in his look of set and passionate
purpose! And that purpose was to kill himself — to be found dead, as his father had
been before him — in an open boat, adrift
upon the Marsh!

It was not the outcome of a sudden fancy.
The idea had first come to him in a taunting
allusion from the drunken lips of one of his
ruder companions, for which he had stricken
the offender to the earth. It had since
haunted his waking hours of remorse and
hopeless fatuity; it had seemed to be the
one relief and atonement he could make his
devoted sister; and, more fatuous than all,
it seemed to the miserable boy the one revenge he would take upon the faithless co-
quette, who for a year had played with his
simplicity, and had helped to drive him to
the distraction of cards and drink. Only

that morning Colonel Preston had forbidden him the house; and now it seemed to him the end had come. He raised his distorted face above the reedy bank for a last tremulous and half-frightened glance at the landscape he was leaving forever. A glint in the western sky lit up the front of his deserted dwelling in the distance, abreast of which the windings of the inlet had unwittingly led him. As he looked he started, and involuntarily dropped into a crouching attitude. For, to his superstitious terror, the sealed windows of his old home were open, the bright panes were glittering with the fading light, and on the outer gallery the familiar figure of his sister stood, as of old, awaiting his return! Was he really going mad, or had this last vision of his former youth been purposely vouchsafed him?

But, even as he gazed, the appearance of another figure in the landscape beyond the house proved the reality of his vision, and as suddenly distracted him from all else. For it was the apparition of a man on horseback approaching the house from the upland; and even at that distance he recognized its well-known outlines. It was Calvert! Calvert the traitor! Calvert, the man whom

he had long suspected as being the secret
lover and destined husband of Cicely Preston! Calvert, who had deceived him with
his calm equanimity and his affected prefer-
ence for Maggie, to conceal his deliberate
understanding with Cicely. What was he
doing here? Was he a double traitor, and
now trying to deceive *her* — as he had him?
And Maggie here! This sudden return —
this preconcerted meeting. It was infamy!

For a moment he remained stupefied, and
then, with a mechanical instinct, plunged his
head and face in the lazy-flowing water, and
then once again rose cool and collected. The
half-mad distraction of his previous resolve
had given way to another, more deliberate,
but not less desperate determination. He
knew now *why* he came there — *why* he had
brought his gun — why his boat had stopped
when it did!

Lying flat in the bottom, he tore away
fragments of the crumbling bank to fill his
frail craft, until he had sunk it to the gun-
wale, and below the low level of the Marsh.
Then, using his hands as noiseless paddles,
he propelled this rude imitation of a floating log slowly past the line of vision, until
the tongue of bushes had hidden him from

view. With a rapid glance at the darkening
flat, he then seized his gun, and springing
to the spongy bank, half crouching half
crawling through reeds and tussocks, he
made his way to the brush. A foot and eye
less experienced would have plunged its
owner helpless in the black quagmire. At
one edge of the thicket he heard hoofs tram-
pling the dried twigs. Calvert's horse was
already there, tied to a skirting alder.

He ran to the house, but, instead of attracting attention by ascending the creaking
steps, made his way to the piles below the
rear gallery and climbed to it noiselessly.
It was the spot where the deserter had ascended a year ago, and, like him, he could
see and hear all that passed distinctly. Calvert stood near the open door as if depart-
ing. Maggie stood between him and the
window, her face in shadow, her hands
clasped tightly behind her. A profound
sadness, partly of the dying day and waning
light, and partly of some vague expiration
of their own sorrow, seemed to encompass
them. Without knowing why, a strange
trembling took the place of James Culpepper's fierce determination, and a film of
moisture stole across his staring eyes.

" When I tell you that I believe all this
will pass, and that you will still win your
brother back to you," said Calvert's sad but
clear voice, " I will tell you why — although,
perhaps, it is only a part of that confidence
you command me to withhold. When I first
saw you, I myself had fallen into like dis-
solute habits ; less excusable than he, for I
had some experience of the world and its
follies. When I met *you*, and fell under
the influence of your pure, simple, and
healthy life ; when I saw that isolation, monotony, misunderstanding, even the sense of
superiority to one's surroundings could be
lived down and triumphed over, without vulgar distractions or pitiful ambitions ; when
I learned to love you — hear me out, Miss
Culpepper, I beg you — you saved *me* — I,
who was nothing to you, even as I honestly
believe you will still save your brother, whom
you love."

" How do you know I did n't *ruin* him ? "
she said, turning upon him bitterly. " How
do you know that it was n't to get rid of *our*
monotony, *our* solitude that I drove him to
this vulgar distraction, this pitiful — yes,
you were right — pitiful ambition ? "

" Because it is n't your real nature," he
said quietly.

" My real nature," she repeated with a half savage vehemence that seemed to be goaded from her by his very gentleness, "my real nature ! What did *he* — what do *you* know of it ? — My real nature ! — I 'll tell you what it was," she went on passionately. " It was to be revenged on you all for your cruelty, your heartlessness, your wickedness to me and mine in the past. It was to pay you off for your slanders of my dead father — for the selfishness that left me and Jim alone with his dead body on the Marsh. That was what sent me to Logport — to get even with you — to — to fool and flaunt you ! There, you have it now ! And now that God has punished me for it by crushing my brother — you — you expect me to let you crush *me* too."

" But," he said eagerly, advancing toward her, " you are wronging me — you are wronging yourself, cruelly."

" Stop," she said, stepping back, with her hands still locked behind her. " Stay where you are. There ! That 's enough ! " She drew herself up and let her hands fall at her side. " Now, let us speak of Jim," she said coldly.

Without seeming to hear her, he regarded her for the first time with hopeless sadness.

" Why did you let my brother believe you were his rival with Cicely Preston ? " she asked impatiently.

" Because I could not undeceive him without telling him I hopelessly loved his sister. You are proud, Miss Culpepper," he said, with the first tinge of bitterness in his even voice. " Can you not understand that others may be proud too ? "

" No," she said bluntly ; " it is not pride but weakness. You could have told him what you knew to be true : that there could be nothing in common between her folk and such savages as we ; that there was a gulf as wide as that Marsh and as black between our natures, our training and theirs, and even if they came to us across it, now and then, to suit their pleasure, light and easy as that tide — it was still there to some day ground and swamp them ! And if he doubted it, you had only to tell him your own story. You had only to tell him what you have just told me — that you yourself, an officer and a gentleman, thought you loved me, a vulgar, uneducated, savage girl, and that I, kinder to you than you to me or him, made you take it back across that tide, because I could n't let you link your life with me, and drag you in the mire."

" You need not have said that, Miss Culpepper," returned Calvert with the same gentle smile, " to prove that I am your inferior
in all but one thing."

" And that ? " she said quickly.

" Is my love."

His gentle face was as set now as her own
as he moved back slowly towards the door.
There he paused.

" You tell me to speak of Jim, and Jim
only. Then hear me. I believe that Miss
Preston cares for him as far as lies in her
young and giddy nature. I could not, therefore, have crushed *his* hope without deceiv-
ing him, for there are as cruel deceits
prompted by what we call reason as by our
love. If you think that a knowledge of this
plain truth would help to save him, I beg
you to be kinder to him than you have been
to me, — or even, let me dare to hope, to
yourself."

He slowly crossed the threshold, still holding his cap lightly in his hand.

" When I tell you that I am going away
to-morrow on a leave of absence, and that in
all probability we may not meet again, you
will not misunderstand why I add my prayer
to the message your friends in Logport

charged me with. They beg that you will give up your idea of returning here, and come back to them. Believe me, you have made yourself loved and respected there, in spite — I beg pardon — perhaps I should say *because* of your pride. Good-night and good-bye."

For a single instant she turned her set face to the window with a sudden convulsive movement, as if she would have called him back, but at the same moment the opposite door creaked and her brother slipped into the room. Whether a quick memory of the deserter's entrance at that door a year ago had crossed her mind, whether there was some strange suggestion in his mud-stained garments and weak deprecating smile, or whether it was the outcome of some desperate struggle within her, there was that in her face that changed his smile into a frightened cry for pardon, as he ran and fell on his knees at her feet. But even as he did so her stern look vanished, and with her arm around him she bent over him and mingled her tears with his.

"I heard it all, Mag dearest! All! Forgive me! I have been crazy! — wild! — I will reform! — I will be better! I will

never disgrace you again, Mag! Never,
never! I swear it!"

She reached down and kissed him. After
a pause, a weak boyish smile struggled into
his face.

"You heard what he said of *her*, Mag. Do
you think it might be true?"

She lifted the damp curls from his forehead with a sad half-maternal smile, but did
not reply.

"And Mag, dear, don't you think *you*
were a little — just a little — hard on *him?*
No! Don't look at me that way, for God's
sake! There, I didn't mean anything. Of
course you knew best. There, Maggie dear,
look up. Hark there! Listen, Mag, do!"

They lifted their eyes to the dim distance
seen through the open door. Borne on the
fading light, and seeming to fall and die
with it over marsh and river, came the last
notes of the bugle from the Fort.

"There! Don't you remember what you
used to say, Mag?"

The look that had frightened him had
quite left her face now.

"Yes," she smiled, laying her cold cheek
beside his softly. "Oh yes! It was something that came and went, 'Like a song' —
'Like a song.'"

A KNIGHT-ERRANT OF THE FOOT-HILLS.

I.

As Father Felipe slowly toiled up the dusty road towards the Rancho of the Blessed Innocents, he more than once stopped under the shadow of a sycamore to rest his somewhat lazy mule and to compose his own perplexed thoughts by a few snatches from his breviary. For the good padre had some reason to be troubled. The invasion of Gentile Americans that followed the gold discovery of three years before had not confined itself to the plains of the Sacramento, but stragglers had already found their way to the Santa Cruz Valley, and the seclusion of even the mission itself was threatened. It was true that they had not brought their heathen engines to disembowel the earth in search of gold, but it was rumored that they had already speculated upon the agricultural productiveness of the land, and had espied

" the fatness thereof." As he reached the higher plateau he could see the afternoon sea-fog — presently to obliterate the fair prospect — already pulling through the gaps in the Coast Range, and on a nearer slope — no less ominously — the smoke of a recent but more permanently destructive Yankee saw-mill was slowly drifting towards the valley.

" Get up, beast!" said the father, digging his heels into the comfortable flanks of his mule with some human impatience, " or art *thou*, too, a lazy renegade? Thinkest thou, besotted one, that the heretic will spare thee more work than the Holy Church."

The mule, thus apostrophized in ear and flesh, shook its head obstinately as if the question was by no means clear to its mind, but nevertheless started into a little trot, which presently brought it to the low adobe wall of the courtyard of " The Innocents," and entered the gate. A few lounging *peons* in the shadow of an archway took off their broad-brimmed hats and made way for the padre, and a half dozen equally listless *vaqueros* helped him to alight. Accustomed as he was to the indolence and superfluity of his host's retainers, to-day it nevertheless seemed to strike some note of irritation in his breast.

A stout, middle-aged woman of ungirt waist and beshawled head and shoulders appeared at the gateway as if awaiting him. After a formal salutation she drew him aside into an inner passage.

"He is away again, your Reverence," she said.

"Ah — always the same?"

"Yes, your Reverence — and this time to 'a meeting' of the heretics at their *pueblo*, at Jonesville — where they will ask him of his land for a road."

"At a *meeting?*" echoed the priest uneasily.

"Ah yes! a meeting — where Tiburcio says they shout and spit on the ground, your Reverence, and only one has a chair and him they call a 'chairman' because of it, and yet he sits not but shouts and spits even as the others and keeps up a tapping with a hammer like a very *pico*. And there it is they are ever 'resolving' that which is not, and consider it even as done."

"Then he is still the same," said the priest gloomily, as the woman paused for breath.

"Only more so, your Reverence, for he reads nought but the newspaper of the *Americanos* that is brought in the ship, the 'New York 'errald' — and recites to himself the orations of their legislators. Ah! it was an evil day when the shipwrecked American sailor taught him his uncouth tongue, which, as your Reverence knows, is only fit for beasts and heathen incantation."

"Pray Heaven *that* were all he learned of him," said the priest hastily, "for I have great fear that this sailor was little better than an atheist and an emissary from Satan. But where are these newspapers and the fantasies of *publicita* that fill his mind? I would see them, my daughter."

"You shall, your Reverence, and more too," she replied eagerly, leading the way along the passage to a grated door which opened upon a small cell-like apartment, whose scant light and less air came through the deeply embayed windows in the outer wall. "Here is his *estudio*."

In spite of this open invitation, the padre entered with that air of furtive and minute inspection common to his order. His glance fell upon a rude surveyor's plan of the adjacent embryo town of Jonesville hanging on the wall, which he contemplated with a cold disfavor that even included the highly colored vignette of the projected Jonesville Hotel in the left-hand corner. He then passed to a supervisor's notice hanging near it, which he examined with a suspicion heightened by that uneasiness common to mere worldly humanity when opposed to an unknown and unfamiliar language. But an exclamation broke from his lips when he confronted an election placard immediately below it. It was printed in Spanish and English, and Father Felipe had no difficulty in reading the announcement that "Don José Sepulvida would preside at a meeting of the Board of Education in Jonesville as one of the trustees."

"This is madness," said the padre.

Observing that Dona Maria was at the moment preoccupied in examining the pictorial pages of an illustrated American weekly which had hitherto escaped his eyes, he took it gently from her hand.

"Pardon, your Reverence," she said with slightly acidulous deprecation, "but thanks to the Blessed Virgin and your Reverence's teaching, the text is but gibberish to me and I did but glance at the pictures."

" Much evil may come in with the eye," said the priest sententiously, " as I will presently show thee. We have here," he continued, pointing to an illustration of certain college athletic sports, " a number of youthful cavaliers posturing and capering in a partly nude condition before a number of shameless women, who emulate the saturnalia of heathen Rome by waving their handkerchiefs. We have here a companion picture," he said, indicating an illustration of gymnastic exercises by the students of a female academy at " Commencement," " in which, as thou seest, even the aged of both sexes unblushingly assist as spectators with every expression of immodest satisfaction."

" Have they no bull-fights or other seemly recreation that they must indulge in such wantonness?" asked Dona Maria indignantly, gazing, however, somewhat curiously at the baleful representations.

" Of all that, my daughter, has their pampered civilization long since wearied," returned the good padre, " for see, this is what they consider a moral and even a religious ceremony." He turned to an illustration of a woman's rights convention; " observe with what rapt attention the audience of that

heathen temple watch the inspired ravings
of that elderly priestess on the dais. It is
even this kind of sacrilegious performance
that I am told thy nephew Don José ex-
pounds and defends."

" May the blessed saints preserve us;
where will it lead to ? " murmured the horri-
fied Dona Maria.

" I will show thee," said Father Felipe,
briskly turning the pages with the same
lofty ignoring of the text until he came to a
representation of a labor procession. " There
is one of their periodic revolutions unhappily
not unknown even in Mexico. Thou per-
ceivest those complacent artisans marching
with implements of their craft, accompanied
by the military, in the presence of their own
stricken masters. Here we see only another
instance of the instability of all communities
that are not founded on the principles of the
Holy Church."

" And what is to be done with my
nephew ? "

The good father's brow darkened with the
gloomy religious zeal of two centuries ago.
" We must have a council of the family, the
alcalde, and the archbishop, at *once*," he said
ominously. To the mere heretical observer

the conclusion might have seemed lame and impotent, but it was as near the Holy Inquisition as the year of grace 1852 could offer.

A few days after this colloquy the unsuspecting subject of it, Don José Sepulvida, was sitting alone in the same apartment. The fading glow of the western sky, through the deep embrasured windows, lit up his rapt and meditative face. He was a young man of apparently twenty-five, with a colorless satin complexion, dark eyes alternating between melancholy and restless energy, a narrow high forehead, long straight hair, and a lightly penciled moustache. He was said to resemble the well-known portrait of the Marquis of Monterey in the mission church, a face that was alleged to leave a deep and lasting impression upon the observers. It was undoubtedly owing to this quality during a brief visit of the famous viceroy to a remote and married ancestress of Don José at Leon that the singular resemblance may be attributed.

A heavy and hesitating step along the passage stopped before the grating. Looking up, Don José beheld to his astonishment the slightly inflamed face of Roberto, a vagabond

American whom he had lately taken into his employment.

Roberto, a polite translation of " Bob the Bucker," cleaned out at a monte-bank in Santa Cruz, penniless and profligate, had sold his mustang to Don José and recklessly thrown himself in with the bargain. · Touched by the rascal's extravagance, the quality of the mare, and observing that Bob's habits had not yet affected his seat in the saddle, but rather lent a demoniac vigor to his chase of wild cattle, Don José had retained rider and horse in his service as *vaquero*.

Bucking Bob, observing that his employer was alone, coolly opened the door without ceremony, shut it softly behind him, and then closed the wooden shutter of the grating. Don José surveyed him with mild surprise and dignified composure. The man appeared perfectly sober, — it was a peculiarity of his dissipated habits that, when not actually raving with drink, he was singularly shrewd and practical.

" Look yer, Don Kosay," he began in a brusque but guarded voice, " you and me is pards. When ye picked me and the mare up and set us on our legs again in this yer ranch, I allowed I 'd tie to ye whenever you was in trouble — and wanted me. And I reckon that's what's the matter now. For from what I see and hear on every side, although you're the boss of this consarn, you're surrounded by a gang of spies and traitors. Your comings and goings, your ins and outs, is dogged and followed and blown upon. The folks you trust is playing it on ye. It ain't for me to say why or wherefore — what's their rights and what's yourn — but I've come to tell ye that if you don't get up and get outer this ranch them d——d priests and **your own** flesh and blood — your aunts and your uncles and your cousins, will have you chucked outer your property, and run into a lunatic asylum."

"Me — Don José Sepulvida — a luna-tico! You are yourself crazy of drink, friend Roberto."

"Yes," said Roberto grimly, "but that kind ain't *illegal*, while your makin' ducks and drakes of your property and going into 'Merikin ideas and 'Merikin speculations they reckon is. And speakin' on the square, it ain't *nat'ral*."

Don José sprang to his feet and began to pace up and down his cell-like study. "Ah, I remember now," he muttered, "I begin to

comprehend : Father Felipe's homilies and
discourses ! My aunt's too affectionate care !
My cousin's discreet consideration ! The
prompt attention of my servants ! I see it
all ! And you," he said, suddenly facing
Roberto, " why come you to tell me this ? "

" Well, boss," said the American dryly,
" I reckoned to stand by you."

" Ah," said Don José, visibly affected.
" Good Roberto, come hither, child, you may
kiss my hand."

" If ! it's all the same to you, Don Kosay,
— *that* kin slide."

" Ah, if — yes," said Don José, meditatively putting his hand to his forehead,
" miserable that I am ! — I remembered not
you were *Americano.* Pardon, my friend —
embrace me — *Conpañero y Amigo.*"

With characteristic gravity he reclined
for a moment upon Robert's astonished
breast. Then recovering himself with equal
gravity he paused, lifted his hand with gentle
warning, marched to a recess in the corner,
unhooked a rapier hanging from the wall,
and turned to his companion.

" We will defend ourselves, friend Roberto. It is the sword of the *Comandante*
— my ancestor. The blade is of Toledo."

" An ordinary six-shooter of Colt's would lay over that," said Roberto grimly — " but that ain't your game just now, Don Kosay. You must get up and get, and at once. You must *vamose* the ranch afore they lay hold of you and have you up before the alcalde. Once away from here, they dare n't follow you where there's 'Merikin law, and when you kin fight 'em in the square."

" Good," said Don José with melancholy preciseness. " You are wise, friend Roberto. We may fight them later, as you say — on the square, or in the open Plaza. And you, *camarado*, *you* shall go with me — you and your mare."

Sincere as the American had been in his offer of service, he was somewhat staggered at this imperative command. But only for a moment. " Well," he said lazily, "I don't care if I do."

" But," said Don José with increased gravity, " you *shall* care, friend Roberto. We shall make an alliance, an union. It is true, my brother, you drink of whiskey, and at such times are even as a madman. It has been recounted to me that it was necessary to your existence that you are a lunatic three days of the week. Who knows? I myself,

though I drink not of *aguardiente*, am ac-
cused of fantasies for all time. Necessary
it becomes therefore that we should go
together. My fantasies and speculations
cannot injure you, my brother ; your whiskey
shall not empoison me. We shall go together in the great world of your American
ideas of which I am much inflamed. We
shall together breathe as one the spirit of
Progress and Liberty. We shall be even
as neophytes making of ourselves Apostles
of Truth. I absolve and renounce myself
henceforth of my family. I shall take to
myself the sister and the brother, the aunt
and the uncle, as we proceed. I devote myself to humanity alone. I devote *you*, my
friend, and the mare — though happily she
has not a Christian soul — to this glorious
mission."

The few level last rays of light lit up a
faint enthusiasm in the face of Don José,
but without altering his imperturbable gravity. The *vaquero* eyed him curiously and
half doubtfully.

" We will go to-morrow," resumed Don
José with solemn decision, " for it is Wednesday. It was a Sunday that thou didst ride
the mare up the steps of the Fonda and de-

manded that thy liquor should be served to thee in a pail. I remember it, for the land-lord of the Fonda claimed twenty *pesos* for damage and the kissing of his wife. There-fore, by computation, good Roberto, thou shouldst be sober until Friday, and we shall have two clear days to fly before thy madness again seizes thee."

"They kin say what they like, Don Ko-say, but *your* head is level," returned the unabashed American, grasping Don José's hand. "All right, then. *Hasta mañana*, as your folks say."

"Hasta mañana," repeated Don José gravely.

At daybreak next morning, while slum-ber still weighted the lazy eyelids of "the Blessed Innocents," Don José Sepulvida and his trusty squire Roberto, otherwise known as "Bucking Bob," rode forth unnoticed from the corral.

II.

THREE days had passed. At the close of the third, Don José was seated in a cosy private apartment of the San Mateo Hotel, where they had halted for an arranged interview with his lawyer before reaching San Francisco. From his window he could see the surrounding park-like avenues of oaks and the level white high road, now and then clouded with the dust of passing teams. But his eyes were persistently fixed upon a small copy of the American Constitution before him. Suddenly there was a quick rap on his door, and before he could reply to it a man brusquely entered.

Don José raised his head slowly, and recognized the landlord. But the intruder, apparently awed by the gentle, grave, and studious figure before him, fell back for an instant in an attitude of surly apology.

"Enter freely, my good Jenkinson," said Don José, with a quiet courtesy that had all the effect of irony. "The apartment, such as it is, is at your disposition. It is even yours, as is the house."

"Well, I'm darned if I know as it is," said the landlord, recovering himself roughly, "and that's jest what's the matter. Yer's that man of yours smashing things right and left in the bar-room and chuckin' my waiters through the window."

"Softly, softly, good Jenkinson," said Don José, putting a mark in the pages of the volume before him. "It is necessary first that I should correct your speech. He is not my '*man*,' which I comprehend to mean a slave, a hireling, a thing obnoxious to the great American nation which *I* admire and to which *he* belongs. Therefore, good Jenkinson, say 'friend,' 'companion,' 'guide,' 'philosopher,' if you will. As to the rest, it is of no doubt as you relate. I myself have heard the breakings of glass and small dishes as I sit here; three times I have seen your waiters projected into the road with much violence and confusion. To myself I have then said, even as I say to you, good Jenkinson, 'Patience, patience, the end is not far.' In four hours," continued Don José, holding up four fingers, "he shall make a finish. Until then, not."

"Well, I 'm d——d," ejaculated Jenkinson, gasping for breath in his indignation.

"Nay, excellent Jenkinson, not dam-ned but of a possibility dam-*aged*. That I shall repay when he have make a finish."

"But, darn it all," broke in the landlord angrily.

"Ah," said Don José gravely, "you would be paid before! Good; for how much shall you value *all* you have in your bar?"

Don José's imperturbability evidently
shook the landlord's faith in the soundness
of his own position. He looked at his guest
critically and audaciously.

"It cost me two hundred dollars to fit it
up," he said curtly.

Don José rose, and, taking a buckskin
purse from his saddle-bag, counted out four
slugs [1] and handed them to the stupefied
Jenkinson. The next moment, however, his
host recovered himself, and casting the slugs
back on the little table, brought his fist
down with an emphasis that made them
dance.

"But, look yer — suppose I want this
thing stopped — you hear me — *stopped* —
now."

"That would be interfering with the liberty of the subject, my good Jenkinson —
which God forbid!" said Don José calmly.
"Moreover, it is the custom of the *Americanos* — a habit of my friend Roberto — a
necessity of his existence — and so recognized of his friends. Patience and courage,
Señor Jenkinson. Stay — ah, I comprehend! you have — of a possibility — a
wife?"

---

[1] Hexagonal gold pieces valued at $50 each, issued by
a private firm as coin in the early days.

"No, I'm a widower," said Jenkinson sharply.

"Then I congratulate you. My friend Roberto would have kissed her. It is also of his habit. Truly you have escaped much. I embrace you, Jenkinson."

He threw his arms gravely around Jenkinson, in whose astounded face at last an expression of dry humor faintly dawned. After a moment's survey of Don José's impenetrable gravity, he coolly gathered up the gold coins, and saying that he would assess the damages and return the difference, he left the room as abruptly as he had entered it.

But Don José was not destined to remain long in peaceful study of the American Constitution. He had barely taken up the book again and renewed his serious contemplation of its excellences when there was another knock at his door. This time, in obedience to his invitation to enter, the new visitor approached with more deliberation and a certain formality.

He was a young man of apparently the same age as Don José, handsomely dressed, and of a quiet self-possession and gravity almost equal to his host's.

"I believe I am addressing Don José

Sepulvida," he said with a familiar yet courteous inclination of his handsome head. Don José, who had risen in marked contrast to his reception of his former guest, answered, —

"You are truly making to him a great honor."

"Well, you're going it blind as far as *I'm* concerned certainly," said the young man, with a slight smile, "for you don't know *me*."

"Pardon, my friend," said Don José gently, "in this book, this great Testament of your glorious nation, I have read that you are all equal, one not above, one not below the other. I salute in you the Nation! It is enough!"

"Thank you," returned the stranger, with a face that, saving the faintest twinkle in the corner of his dark eyes, was as immovable as his host's, "but for the purposes of my business I had better say I am Jack Hamlin, a gambler, and am just now dealing faro in the Florida saloon round the corner."

He paused carelessly, as if to allow Don José the protest he did not make, and then continued, —

"The matter is this. One of your *vaque-*

ros, who is, however, an American, was round there an hour ago bucking against faro, and put up and *lost*, not only the mare he was riding, but a horse which I have just learned is yours. Now we reckon, over there, that we can make enough money playing a square game, without being obliged to take property from a howling drunkard, to say nothing of it not belonging to him, and I've come here, Don José, to say that if you'll send over and bring away your man and your horse, you can have 'em both."

"If I have comprehended, honest Hamlin," said Don José slowly, "this Roberto, who was my *vaquero* and is my brother, has approached this faro game by himself unsolicited?"

"He certainly did n't seem shy of it," said Mr. Hamlin with equal gravity. "To the best of my knowledge he looked as if he 'd been there before."

"And if he had won, excellent Hamlin, you would have given him the equal of his mare and horse?"

"A hundred dollars for each, yes, certainly."

"Then I see not why I should send for the property which is truly no longer mine,

nor for my brother who will amuse himself
after the fashion of his country in the company of so honorable a *caballero* as yourself? Stay! oh imbecile that I am. I have
not remembered. You would possibly say
that he has no longer of horses! Play him;
play him, admirable yet prudent Hamlin. I
have two thousand horses! Of a surety he
cannot exhaust them in four hours. Therefore play him, trust to me for *recompensa*,
and have no fear."

A quick flush covered the stranger's
cheek, and his eyebrows momentarily contracted. He walked carelessly to the window, however, glanced out, and then turned
to Don José.

"May I ask, then," he said with almost
sepulchral gravity, " is anybody taking care
of you?"

"Truly," returned Don José cautiously,
"there is my brother and friend Roberto."

"Ah! Roberto, certainly," said Mr. Hamlin profoundly.

"Why do you ask, considerate friend?"

"Oh! I only thought, with your kind of
opinions, you must often feel lonely in Cali-
fornia. Good-bye." He shook Don José's
hand heartily, took up his hat, inclined his

head with graceful seriousness, and passed out of the room. In the hall he met the landlord.

"Well," said Jenkinson, with a smile half anxious, half insinuating, "you saw him? What do you think of him?"

Mr. Hamlin paused and regarded Jenkinson with a calmly contemplative air, as if he were trying to remember first who he was, and secondly why he should speak to him at all. "Think of whom?" he repeated carelessly.

"Why him — you know — Don José."

"I did not see anything the matter with him," returned Hamlin with frigid simplicity.

"What? nothing queer?"

"Well, no — except that he's a guest in *your* house," said Hamlin with great cheerfulness. "But then, as you keep a hotel, you can't help occasionally admitting a — gentleman."

Mr. Jenkinson smiled the uneasy smile of a man who knew that his interlocutor's playfulness occasionally extended to the use of a derringer, in which he was singularly prompt and proficient, and Mr. Hamlin, equally conscious of that knowledge on the part of his companion, descended the staircase composedly.

But the day had darkened gradually into night, and Don José was at last compelled to put aside his volume. The sound of a large bell rung violently along the hall and passages admonished him that the American dinner was ready, and although the viands and the mode of cooking were not entirely to his fancy, he had, in his grave enthusiasm for the national habits, attended the *table d'hôte* regularly with Roberto. On reaching the lower hall he was informed that his henchman had early succumbed to the potency of his libations, and had already been carried by two men to bed. Receiving this information with his usual stoical composure, he entered the dining-room, but was surprised to find that a separate table had been prepared for him by the landlord, and that a rude attempt had been made to serve him with his own native dishes.

"Señores y Señoritas," said Don José, turning from it and with grave politeness addressing the assembled company, " if I seem to-day to partake alone and in a reserved fashion of certain viands that have been prepared for me, it is truly from no lack of courtesy to your distinguished company, but rather, I protest, to avoid the appearance of greater discourtesy to our excellent Jenkinson, who has taken some pains and trouble to comport his establishment to what he conceives to be my desires. Wherefore, my friends, in God's name fall to, the same as if I were not present, and grace be with you."

A few stared at the tall, gentle, melancholy figure with some astonishment; a few whispered to their neighbors; but when, at the conclusion of his repast, Don José arose and again saluted the company, one or two stood up and smilingly returned the courtesy, and Polly Jenkinson, the landlord's youngest daughter, to the great delight of her companions, blew him a kiss.

After visiting the *vaquero* in his room, and with his own hand applying some native ointment to the various contusions and scratches which recorded the late engagements of the unconscious Roberto, Don José placed a gold coin in the hands of the Irish chamber-maid, and bidding her look after the sleeper, he threw his *serape* over his shoulders and passed into the road. The loungers on the veranda gazed at him curiously, yet half acknowledged his usual se-

rious salutation, and made way for him with
a certain respect. Avoiding the few narrow
streets of the little town, he pursued his way
meditatively along the highroad, returning
to the hotel after an hour's ramble, as the
evening stage-coach had deposited its passengers and departed.

"There's a lady waiting to see you upstairs," said the landlord with a peculiar
smile. "She rather allowed it was n't the
proper thing to see you alone, or she was n't
quite ekal to it, I reckon, for she got my
Polly to stand by her."

"Your Polly, good Jenkinson?" said Don
José interrogatively.

"My darter, Don José."

"Ah, truly! I am twice blessed," said
Don José, gravely ascending the staircase.

On entering the room he perceived a tall,
large-featured woman with an extraordinary
quantity of blond hair parted on one side of
her broad forehead, sitting upon the sofa.
Beside her sat Polly Jenkinson, her fresh,
honest, and rather pretty face beaming with
delighted expectation and mischief. Don
José saluted them with a formal courtesy,
which, however, had no trace of the fact that
he really did not remember anything of
them.

" I called," said the large-featured woman with a voice equally pronounced, " in reference to a request from you, which, though perhaps unconventional in the extreme, I have been able to meet by the intervention of this young lady's company. My name on this card may not be familiar to you — but I am 'Dorothy Dewdrop.' "

A slight movement of abstraction and surprise passed over Don José's face, but as quickly vanished as he advanced towards her and gracefully raised the tips of her fingers to his lips. " Have I then, at last, the privilege of beholding that most distressed and deeply injured of women! Or is it but a dream ! "

It certainly was not, as far as concerned the substantial person of the woman before him, who, however, seemed somewhat uneasy under his words as well as the demure scrutiny of Miss Jenkinson. "I thought you might have forgotten," she said with slight acerbity, " that you desired an interview with the authoress of " —

" Pardon," interrupted Don José, standing before her in an attitude of the deepest sympathizing dejection, "I had not forgotten. It is now three weeks since I have

read in the journal 'Golden Gate' the eloquent and touching poem of your sufferings,
and your aspirations, and your miscompre-
hensions by those you love. I remember as
yesterday that you have said, that cruel fate
have linked you to a soulless state — that —
but I speak not well your own beautiful language — you are in tears at evenfall ' because
that you are not understood of others, and
that your soul recoiled from iron bonds, until, as in a dream, you sought succor and re-
lease in some true Knight of equal plight.' "

"I am told," said the large featured woman with some satisfaction, "that the poem
to which you allude has been generally admired."

"Admired! Señora," said Don José, with
still darker sympathy, "it is not the word ;
it is *felt.* I have felt it. When I read those
words of distress, I am touched of compas-
sion! I have said, This woman, so disconsolate, so oppressed, must be relieved, pro-
tected! I have wrote to you, at the 'Golden
Gate,' to see me here."

"And I have come, as you perceive," said
the poetess, rising with a slight smile of con-
straint; "and emboldened by your appreciation, I have brought a few trifles thrown
off " —

" Pardon, unhappy Señora," interrupted Don José, lifting his hand deprecatingly without relaxing his melancholy precision, "but to a cavalier further evidence is not required — and I have not yet make finish. I have not content myself to *write* to you. I have sent my trusty friend Roberto to inquire at the ' Golden Gate ' of your condition. I have found there, most unhappy and persecuted friend — that with truly angelic forbearance you have not told *all* — that you are *married*, and that of a necessity it is your husband that is cold and soulless and unsympathizing — and all that you describe."

" Sir ! " said the poetess, rising in angry consternation.

" I have written to him," continued Don José, with unheeding gravity ; " have appealed to him as a friend, I have conjured him as a *caballero*, I have threatened him even as a champion of the Right, I have said to him, in effect — that this must not be as it is. I have informed him that I have made an appointment with you even at this house, and I challenged him to meet you here — in this room — even at this instant, and, with God's help, we should make good

our charges against him. It is yet early; I
have allowed time for the lateness of the
stage and the fact that he will come by another conveyance. Therefore, O Dona Dewdrop, tremble not like thy namesake as it
were on the leaf of apprehension and expec-
tancy. I, Don José, am here to protect thee.
I will take these charges " — gently withdrawing the manuscripts from her astonished
grasp — " though even, as I related to thee
before, I want them not, yet we will together
confront him with them and make them
good against him."

" Are you mad ? " demanded the lady in
almost stentorious accents, " or is this an
unmanly hoax ? " Suddenly she stopped in
undeniable consternation. " Good heavens,"
she muttered, " if Abner should believe this.
He is *such* a fool ! He has lately been
queer and jealous. Oh dear ! " she said,
turning to Polly Jenkinson with the first indication of feminine weakness, " *is* he telling the truth ? is he crazy ? what shall I do ? "

Polly Jenkinson, who had witnessed the
interview with the intensest enjoyment, now
rose equal to the occasion.

" You have made a mistake," she said, uplifting her demure blue eyes to Don José's

dark and melancholy gaze. "This lady is a *poetess!* The sufferings she depicts, the sorrows she feels, are in the *imagination*, in her fancy only."

"Ah!" said Don José gloomily; "then it is all false."

"No," said Polly quickly, "only they are not her *own*, you know. They are somebody elses. She only describes them for another, don't you see?"

"And who, then, is this unhappy one?" asked the Don quickly.

"Well — a — friend," stammered Polly, hesitatingly.

"A friend!" repeated Don José. "Ah, I see, of possibility a dear one, even," he continued, gazing with tender melancholy into the untroubled cerulean depths of Polly's eyes, "even, but no, child, it could not be! *thou* art too young."

"Ah," said Polly, with an extraordinary gulp and a fierce nudge of the poetess, "but it *was* me."

"You, Señorita," repeated Don José, falling back in an attitude of mingled admiration and pity. "You, the child of Jenkinson!"

"Yes, yes," joined in the poetess hurriedly; " but that isn't going to stop the consequences of your wretched blunder. My husband will be furious, and will be here at any moment. Good gracious! what is that?"

The violent slamming of a distant door at that instant, the sounds of quick scuffling on the staircase, and the uplifting of an irate voice had reached her ears and thrown her back in the arms of Polly Jenkinson. Even the young girl herself turned an anxious gaze towards the door. Don José alone was unmoved.

"Possess yourselves in peace, Señoritas," he said calmly. "We have here only the characteristic convalescence of my friend and brother, the excellent Roberto. He will ever recover himself from drink with violence, even as he precipitates himself into it with fury. He has been prematurely awakened. I will discover the cause."

With an elaborate bow to the frightened women, he left the room. Scarcely had the door closed when the poetess turned quickly to Polly. "The man's a stark staring lunatic, but, thank Heaven, Abner will see it at once. And now let's get away while we can. To think," she said, snatching up her scattered manuscripts, "that *that* was all the beast wanted."

" I 'm sure he 's very gentle and kind," said Polly, recovering her dimples with a demure pout; " but stop, he 's coming back."

It was indeed Don José re-entering the room with the composure of a relieved and self-satisfied mind. "It is even as I said, Señora," he began, taking the poetess's hand, — " and *more.* You are *saved !* "

As the women only stared at each other, he gravely folded his arms and continued : " I will explain. For the instant I have not remember that, in imitation of your own delicacy, I have given to your husband in my letter, not the name of myself, but, as a mere *Don Fulano,* the name of my brother Roberto — ' Bucking Bob.' Your husband have this moment arrive ! Penetrating the bedroom of the excellent Roberto, he has indiscreetly seize him in his bed, without explanation, without introduction, without fear ! The excellent Roberto, ever ready for such distractions, have respond ! In a word, to use the language of the good Jenkinson — our host, our father — who was present, he have ' wiped the floor with your husband,' and have even carried him down the staircase to the street. Believe me, he will not return. You are free ! "

"Fool! Idiot! Crazy beast!" said the poetess, dashing past him and out of the door. "You shall pay for this!"

Don José did not change his imperturbable and melancholy calm. "And now, little one," he said, dropping on one knee before the half-frightened Polly, "child of Jenkinson, now that thy perhaps too excitable sponsor has, in a poet's caprice, abandoned thee for some newer fantasy, confide in me thy distress, to me, thy Knight, and tell the story of thy sorrows."

"But," said Polly, rising to her feet and struggling between a laugh and a cry. "I have n't any sorrows. Oh dear! don't you see, it's only her *fancy* to make me seem so. There's nothing the matter with me."

"Nothing the matter," repeated Don José slowly. "You have no distress? You want no succor, no relief, no protector? This, then, is but another delusion!" he said, rising sadly.

"Yes, no — that is — oh, my gracious goodness!" said Polly, hopelessly divided between a sense of the ridiculous and some strange attraction in the dark, gentle eyes that were fixed upon her half reproachfully. "You don't understand."

Don José replied only with a melancholy smile, and then going to the door, opened it with a bowed head and respectful courtesy. At the act, Polly plucked up courage again, and with it a slight dash of her old audacity.

"I'm sure I'm very sorry that I ain't got any love sorrows," she said demurely. "And I suppose it's very dreadful in me not to have been raving and broken-hearted over somebody or other as that woman has said. Only," she waited till she had gained the secure vantage of the threshold, "I never knew a gentleman to *object* to it before!"

With this Parthian arrow from her blue eyes she slipped into the passage and vanished through the door of the opposite parlor. For an instant Don José remained motionless and reflecting. Then, recovering himself with grave precision, he deliberately picked up his narrow black gloves from the table, drew them on, took his hat in his hand, and solemnly striding across the passage, entered the door that had just closed behind her.

III.

It must not be supposed that in the meantime the flight of Don José and his follower

was unattended by any commotion at the
rancho of the Blessed Innocents. At the
end of three hours' deliberation, in which the
retainers were severally examined, the corral
searched, and the well in the courtyard
sounded, scouts were dispatched in different
directions, who returned with the surprising
information that the fugitives were not in
the vicinity. A trustworthy messenger was
sent to Monterey for " custom-house paper,"
on which to draw up a formal declaration of
the affair. The archbishop was summoned
from San Luis,· and Don Victor and Don
Vincente Sepulvida, with the Donas Carmen
and Inez Alvarado, and a former alcalde,
gathered at a family council the next day.
In this serious conclave the good Father
Felipe once more expounded the alienated
condition and the dangerous reading of the
absent man. In the midst of which the ordinary post brought a letter from Don José,
calmly inviting the family to dine with him
and Roberto at San Mateo on the following
Wednesday. The document was passed
gravely from hand to hand. Was it a fresh
evidence of mental aberration — an audacity
of frenzy — or a trick of the *vaquero?* The
archbishop and alcalde shook their heads

— it was without doubt a lawless, even a sacrilegious and blasphemous *fête*. But a certain curiosity of the ladies and of Father Felipe carried the day. Without formally accepting the invitation it was decided that the family should examine the afflicted man, with a view of taking active measures here-after. On the day appointed, the traveling carriage of the Sepulvidas, an equipage co-eval with the beginning of the century, drawn by two white mules gaudily capari-soned, halted before the hotel at San Mateo and disgorged Father Felipe, the Donas Car-men and Inez Alvarado and Maria Sepul-vida, while Don Victor and Don Vincente Sepulvida, their attendant cavaliers on fiery mustangs, like outriders, drew rein at the same time. A slight thrill of excitement, as of the advent of a possible circus, had pre-ceded them through the little town; a faint blending of cigarette smoke and garlic an-nounced their presence on the veranda.

Ushered into the parlor of the hotel, ap-parently set apart for their reception, they were embarrassed at not finding their host present. But they were still more discon-certed when a tall full-bearded stranger, with a shrewd amused-looking face, rose from a chair by the window, and stepping forward, saluted them in fluent Spanish with a slight American accent.

"I have to ask you, gentlemen and ladies," he began, with a certain insinuating ease and frankness that alternately aroused and lulled their suspicions, "to pardon the absence of our friend Don José Sepulvida at this preliminary greeting. For to be perfectly frank with you, although the ultimate aim and object of our gathering is a social one, you are doubtless aware that certain infelicities and misunderstandings — common to most families — have occurred, and a free, dispassionate, unprejudiced discussion and disposal of them at the beginning will only tend to augment the goodwill of our gathering."

"The Señor without doubt is" — suggested the padre, with a polite interrogative pause.

"Pardon me! I forgot to introduce myself. Colonel Parker — entirely at your service and that of these charming ladies."

The ladies referred to allowed their eyes to rest with evident prepossession on the insinuating stranger. "Ah, a soldier," said Don Vincente.

"Formerly," said the American lightly; "at present a lawyer, the counsel of Don José."

A sudden rigor of suspicion stiffened the company; the ladies withdrew their eyes; the priest and the Sepulvidas exchanged glances.

"Come," said Colonel Parker, with apparent unconsciousness of the effect of his disclosure, "let us begin frankly. You have, I believe, some anxiety in regard to the mental condition of Don José."

"We believe him to be mad," said Padre Felipe promptly, "irresponsible, possessed!"

"That is your opinion; good," said the lawyer quietly.

"And ours too," clamored the party, "without doubt."

"Good," returned the lawyer with perfect cheerfulness. "As his relations, you have no doubt had superior opportunities for observing his condition. I understand also that you may think it necessary to have him legally declared *non compos*, a proceeding which, you are aware, might result in the incarceration of our distinguished friend in a mad-house."

"Pardon, Señor," interrupted Dona Maria

proudly, "you do not comprehend the family.
When a Sepulvida is visited of God we do
not ask the Government to confine him like
a criminal. We protect him in his own
house from the consequences of his frenzy."

"From the machinations of the worldly
and heretical," broke in the priest, "and
from the waste and dispersion of inherited
possessions."

"Very true," continued Colonel Parker,
with unalterable good-humor; "but I was
only about to say that there might be conflicting evidence of his condition. For instance, our friend has been here three days.
In that time he has had three interviews
with three individuals under singular circumstances." Colonel Parker then briefly recounted the episodes of the landlord, the
gambler, Miss Jenkinson and the poetess, as
they had been related to him. "Yet," he
continued, "all but one of these individuals
are willing to swear that they not only believe Don José perfectly sane, but endowed
with a singularly sound judgment. In fact,
the testimony of Mr. Hamlin and Miss Jenkinson is remarkably clear on that subject."

The company exchanged a supercilious
smile. "Do you not see, O Señor Advo-

cate," said Don Vincente compassionately, " that this is but a conspiracy to avail themselves of our relative's weakness. Of a necessity they find him sane who benefits them."

" I have thought of that, and am glad to hear you say so," returned the lawyer still more cheerfully, " for your prompt opinion emboldens me to be at once perfectly frank with you. Briefly then, Don José has summoned me here to make a final disposition of his property. In the carrying out of certain theories of his, which it is not my province to question, he has resolved upon comparative poverty for himself as best fitted for his purpose, and to employ his wealth solely for others. In fact, of all his vast possessions he retains for himself only an income sufficient for the bare necessaries of life."

" And you have done this? " they asked in one voice.

" Not yet," said the lawyer.

" Blessed San Antonio, we have come in time!" ejaculated Dona Carmen. " Another day and it would have been too late; it was an inspiration of the Blessed Innocents themselves," said Dona Maria, crossing herself. " Can you longer doubt that this is

the wildest madness?" said Father Felipe
with flashing eyes.

"Yet," returned the lawyer, caressing his
heavy beard with a meditative smile, "the
ingenious fellow actually instanced the vows
of *your own order*, reverend sir, as an example in support of his theory. But to be
brief. Conceiving, then, that his holding
of property was a mere accident of heri-
tage, not admitted by him, unworthy his acceptance, and a relic of superstitious ignorance " —

"This is the very sacrilege of Satanic prepossession," broke in the priest indignantly.

"He therefore," continued the lawyer
composedly, "makes over and reverts the
whole of his possessions, with the exceptions
I have stated, to his family and the Church."

A breathless and stupefying silence fell
upon the company. In the dead hush the
sound of Polly Jenkinson's piano, played in
a distant room, could be distinctly heard.
With their vacant eyes staring at him the
speaker continued :

"That deed of gift I have drawn up as he
dictated it. I don't mind saying that in the
opinion of some he might be declared *non
compos* upon the evidence of that alone. I

need not say how relieved I am to find that
your opinion coincides with my own."

"But," gasped Father Felipe hurriedly,
with a quick glance at the others, "it does
not follow that it will be necessary to resort
to these legal measures. Care, counsel, per-
suasion — "

"The general ministering of kinship —
nursing, a woman's care — the instincts of
affection," piped Dona Maria in breathless
eagerness.

"Any light social distraction — a harmless flirtation — a possible attachment," suggested Dona Carmen shyly.

"Change of scene — active exercise — ex-
periences — even as those you have related,"
broke in Don Vincente.

"I for one have ever been opposed to *legal*
measures," said Don Victor. "A mere con-
sultation of friends — in fact, a *fête* like this
is sufficient."

"Good friends," said Father Felipe, who
had by this time recovered himself, taking
out his snuff-box portentously, "it would
seem truly, from the document which this
discreet *caballero* has spoken of, that the
errors of our dear Don José are rather of
method than intent, and that while we may
freely accept the one " —

" Pardon," interrupted Colonel Parker with bland persistence, " but I must point out to you that what we call in law ' a consideration ' is necessary to the legality of a conveyance, even though that consideration be frivolous and calculated to impair the validity of the document."

" Truly," returned the good padre insinuatingly ; " but if a discreet advocate were to suggest the substitution of some more pious and reasonable consideration " —

" But that would be making it a perfectly sane and gratuitous document, not only glaringly inconsistent with your charges, my good friends, with Don José's attitude towards you and his flight from home, but open to the gravest suspicion in law. In fact, its apparent propriety in the face of these facts would imply improper influence."

The countenances of the company fell. The lawyer's face, however, became still more good-humored and sympathizing. " The case is simply this. If in the opinion of judge and jury Don José is declared insane, the document is worthless except as a proof of that fact or a possible indication of the undue influence of his relations, which might compel the court to select his guardians and trustees elsewhere than among them."

"Friend Abogado," said Father Felipe
with extraordinary deliberation, "the document thou hast just described so eloquently
convinces me beyond all doubt that Don
José is not only perfectly sane but endowed
with a singular discretion. I consider it as
a delicate and high-spirited intimation to us,
his friends and kinsmen, of his unalterable
and logically just devotion to his family and
religion, whatever may seem to be his poeti-
cal and imaginative manner of declaring it.
I think there is not one here," continued the
padre, looking around him impressively,
"who is not entirely satisfied of Don José's
reason and competency to arrange his own
affairs."

"Entirely," "truly," "perfectly," eagerly
responded the others with affecting spon-
taneity.

"Nay, more. To prevent any misconcep-
tion, we shall deem it our duty to take every
opportunity of making our belief publicly
known," added Father Felipe.

The padre and Colonel Parker gazed long
and gravely into each other's eyes. It may
have been an innocent touch of the sunlight
through the window, but a faint gleam
seemed to steal into the pupil of the affable

lawyer at the same moment that, probably from the like cause, there was a slight nervous contraction of the left eyelid of the pious father. But it passed, and the next instant the door opened to admit Don José Sepulvida.

He was at once seized and effusively embraced by the entire company with every protest of affection and respect. Not only Mr. Hamlin and Mr. Jenkinson, who accompanied him as invited guests, but Roberto, in a new suit of clothes and guiltless of stain or trace of dissipation, shared in the pronounced friendliness of the kinsmen. Padre Felipe took snuff, Colonel Parker blew his nose gently.

Nor were they less demonstrative of their new convictions later at the banquet. Don José, with Jenkinson and the padre on his right and left, preserved his gentle and half-melancholy dignity in the midst of the noisy fraternization. Even Padre Felipe, in a brief speech or exhortation proposing the health of their host, lent himself in his own tongue to this polite congeniality. "We have had also, my friends and brothers," he said in peroration, "a pleasing example of the compliment of imitation shown by our beloved Don José. No one who has known him during his friendly sojourn in this community but will be struck with the conviction that he has acquired that most marvelous faculty of your great American nation, the exhibition of humor and of the practical joke."

Every eye was turned upon the imperturbable face of Don José as he slowly rose to reply. " In bidding you to this *fête*, my friends and kinsmen," he began calmly, " it was with the intention of formally embracing the habits, customs, and spirit of American institutions by certain methods of renunciation of the past, as became a *caballero* of honor and resolution. Those methods may possibly be known to some of you." He paused for a moment as if to allow the members of his family to look unconscious. " Since then, in the wisdom of God, it has occurred to me that my purpose may be as honorably effected by a discreet blending of the past and the present — in a word, by the judicious combination of the interests of my native people and the American nation. In consideration of that purpose, friends and kinsmen, I ask you to join me in drinking the good health of my host Señor Jenkinson,

my future father-in-law, from whom I have
to-day had the honor to demand the hand
of the peerless Polly, his daughter, as the
future mistress of the Rancho of the Blessed
Innocents."

The marriage took place shortly after.
Nor was the free will and independence of
Don José Sepulvida in the least opposed by
his relations. Whether they felt they had
already committed themselves, or had hopes
in the future, did not transpire. Enough
that the escapade of a week was tacitly forgotten. The only allusion ever made to the
bridegroom's peculiarities was drawn from
the demure lips of the bride herself on her
installation at the "Blessed Innocents."

"And what, little one, didst thou find in
me to admire?" Don José had asked tenderly.

"Oh, you seemed to be so much like that
dear old Don Quixote, you know," she answered demurely.

"Don Quixote," repeated Don José with
gentle gravity. "But, my child, that was
only a mere fiction — a romance, of one Cer-
vantes. Believe me, of a truth there never
was any such person!"

A SECRET OF TELEGRAPH HILL.

I.

As Mr. Herbert Bly glanced for the first
time at the house which was to be his future
abode in San Francisco, he was somewhat
startled. In that early period of feverish
civic improvement the street before it had
been repeatedly graded and lowered until
the dwelling — originally a pioneer suburban
villa perched upon a slope of Telegraph Hill
— now stood sixty feet above the sidewalk,
superposed like some Swiss châlet on succes-
sive galleries built in the sand-hill, and con-
nected by a half-dozen distinct zigzag flights
of wooden staircase. Stimulated, however,
by the thought that the view from the top
would be a fine one, and that existence there
would have all the quaint originality of Rob-
inson Crusoe's tree-dwelling, Mr. Bly began
cheerfully to mount the steps. It should be
premised that, although a recently appointed
clerk in a large banking house, Mr. Bly was

somewhat youthful and imaginative, and regarded the ascent as part of that "Excelsior" climbing pointed out by a great poet as
a praiseworthy function of ambitious youth.

Reaching at last the level of the veranda,
he turned to the view. The distant wooded
shore of Contra Costa, the tossing white-caps
and dancing sails of the bay between, and
the foreground at his feet of wharves and
piers, with their reed-like jungles of masts
and cordage, made up a bright, if somewhat
material, picture. To his right rose the crest
of the hill, historic and memorable as the site
of the old semaphoric telegraph, the tossing
of whose gaunt arms formerly thrilled the
citizens with tidings from the sea. Turning
to the house, he recognized the prevailing style of light cottage architecture, although incongruously confined to narrow
building plots and the civic regularity of a
precise street frontage. Thus a dozen other
villas, formerly scattered over the slope, had
been laboriously displaced and moved to the
rigorous parade line drawn by the street surveyor, no matter how irregular and independent their design and structure. Happily,
the few scrub-oaks and low bushes which
formed the scant vegetation of this vast sand

dune offered no obstacle and suggested no incongruity. Beside the house before which Mr. Bly now stood, a prolific Madeira vine, quickened by the six months' sunshine, had alone survived the displacement of its foundations, and in its untrimmed luxuriance half hid the upper veranda from his view.

Still glowing with his exertion, the young man rang the bell and was admitted into a fair-sized drawing-room, whose tasteful and well-arranged furniture at once prepossessed him. An open piano, a sheet of music carelessly left on the stool, a novel lying face downwards on the table beside a skein of silk, and the distant rustle of a vanished skirt through an inner door, gave a suggestion of refined domesticity to the room that touched the fancy of the homeless and nomadic Bly. He was still enjoying, in half embarrassment, that vague and indescribable atmosphere of a refined woman's habitual presence, when the door opened and the mistress of the house formally presented herself.

She was a faded but still handsome woman. Yet she wore that peculiar long, limp, formless house-shawl which in certain phases of Anglo-Saxon spinster and widowhood assumes the functions of the recluse's veil and announces the renunciation of worldly vanities and a resigned indifference to external feminine contour. The most audacious masculine arm would shrink from clasping that shapeless void in which the flatness of asceticism or the heavings of passion might alike lie buried. She had also in some mysterious way imported into the fresh and pleasant room a certain bombaziny shadow of the past, and a suggestion of that appalling reminiscence known as " better days." Though why it should be always represented by ashen memories, or why better days in the past should be supposed to fix their fitting symbol in depression in the present, Mr. Bly was too young and too preoccupied at the moment to determine. He only knew that he was a little frightened of her, and fixed his gaze with a hopeless fascination on a letter which she somewhat portentously carried under the shawl, and which seemed already to have yellowed in its arctic shade.

" Mr. Carstone has written to me that you would call," said Mrs. Brooks with languid formality. " Mr. Carstone was a valued friend of my late husband, and I suppose has told you the circumstances — the only circumstances — which admit of my entertaining his proposition of taking anybody, even temporarily, under my roof. The absence of my dear son for six months at Portland, Oregon, enables me to place his room at the disposal of Mr. Carstone's young protégé, who, Mr. Carstone tells me, and I have every reason to believe, is, if perhaps not so seriously inclined nor yet a church communicant, still of a character and reputation not unworthy to follow my dear Tappington in our little family circle as he has at his desk in the bank."

The sensitive Bly, struggling painfully out of an abstraction as to how he was ever to offer the weekly rent of his lodgings to such a remote and respectable person, and also somewhat embarrassed at being appealed to in the third person, here started and bowed.

"The name of Bly is not unfamiliar to me," continued Mrs. Brooks, pointing to a chair and sinking resignedly into another, where her baleful shawl at once assumed the appearance of a dust-cover; "some of my dearest friends were intimate with the Blys of Philadelphia. They were a branch of the Maryland Blys of the eastern shore, one of whom my Uncle James married. Perhaps you are distantly related ? "

Mrs. Brooks was perfectly aware that her
visitor was of unknown Western origin, and
a poor but clever protégé of the rich banker ;
but she was one of a certain class of American women who, in the midst of a fierce
democracy, are more or less cat-like conser-
vators of family pride and lineage, and more
or less felinely inconsistent and treacherous
to republican principles. Bly, who had just
settled in his mind to send her the rent
anonymously — as a weekly valentine — recovered himself and his spirits in his usual
boyish fashion.

"I am afraid, Mrs. Brooks," he said gayly,
"I cannot lay claim to any distinguished
relationship, even to that 'Nelly Bly' who,
you remember, 'winked her eye when she
went to sleep.'" He stopped in consternation. The terrible conviction flashed upon
him that this quotation from a popular
negro-minstrel song could not possibly be remembered by a lady as refined as his host-
ess, or even known to her superior son. The
conviction was intensified by Mrs. Brooks
rising with a smileless face, slightly shedding
the possible vulgarity with a shake of her
shawl, and remarking that she would show
him her son's room, led the way upstairs to

the apartment recently vacated by the perfect Tappington.

Preceded by the same distant flutter of
unseen skirts in the passage which he had
first noticed on entering the drawing-room,
and which evidently did not proceed from
his companion, whose self-composed cerements would have repressed any such indecorous agitation, Mr. Bly stepped timidly
into the room.   It was a very pretty apartment, suggesting the same touches of tasteful refinement in its furniture and appointments, and withal so feminine in its neatness and regularity, that, conscious of his
frontier habits and experience, he felt at
once repulsively incongruous.   "I cannot
expect, Mr. Bly," said Mrs. Brooks resignedly, "that you can share my son's extreme
sensitiveness to disorder and irregularity;
but I must beg you to avoid as much as
possible disturbing the arrangement of the
book-shelves, which, you observe, comprise
his books of serious reference, the Biblical
commentaries, and the sermons which were
his habitual study.   I must beg you to exercise the same care in reference to the valuable offerings from his Sabbath-school scholars
which are upon the mantel.   The embroi-

dered book-marker, the gift of the young ladies of his Bible-class in Dr. Stout's church,
is also, you perceive, kept for ornament and
affectionate remembrance. The harmonium
— even if you are not yourself given to sacred song — I trust you will not find in your
way, nor object to my daughter continuing
her practice during your daily absence.
Thank you. The door you are looking at
leads by a flight of steps to the side street."

"A very convenient arrangement," said
Bly hopefully, who saw a chance for an
occasional unostentatious escape from a too
protracted contemplation of Tappington's
perfections. "I mean," he added hurriedly,
"to avoid disturbing you at night."

"I believe my son had neither the necessity nor desire to use it for that purpose,"
returned Mrs. Brooks severely; "although
he found it sometimes a convenient short cut
to church on Sabbath when he was late."

Bly, who in his boyish sensitiveness to
external impressions had by this time concluded that a life divided between the past
perfections of Tappington and the present
renunciations of Mrs. Brooks would be intolerable, and was again abstractedly invent-
ing some delicate excuse for withdrawing

without committing himself further, was here
suddenly attracted by a repetition of the
rustling of the unseen skirt. This time it
was nearer, and this time it seemed to strike
even Mrs. Brooks's remote preoccupation.
" My daughter, who is deeply devoted to her
brother," she said, slightly raising her voice,
" will take upon herself the care of looking
after Tappington's precious mementoes, and
spare you the trouble. Cherry, dear! this
way. This is the young gentleman spoken
of by Mr. Carstone, your papa's friend. My
daughter Cherubina, Mr. Bly."

The fair owner of the rustling skirt, which
turned out to be a pretty French print, had
appeared at the doorway. She was a tall,
slim blonde, with a shy, startled manner, as
of a penitent nun who was suffering for some
conventual transgression — a resemblance
that was heightened by her short-cut hair,
that might have been cropped as if for punishment. A certain likeness to her mother
suggested that she was qualifying for that
saint's ascetic shawl — subject, however, to
rebellious intervals, indicated in the occasional sidelong fires of her gray eyes. Yet
the vague impression that she knew more of
the world than her mother, and that she did

not look at all as if her name was Cherubina, struck Bly in the same momentary glance.

" Mr. Bly is naturally pleased with what he has seen of our dear Tappington's appointments; and as I gather from Mr. Carstone's letter that he is anxious to enter at once and make the most of the dear boy's absence, you will see, my dear Cherry, that Ellen has everything ready for him ? "

Before the unfortunate Bly could explain or protest, the young girl lifted her gray eyes to his. Whether she had perceived and understood his perplexity he could not tell ; but the swift shy glance was at once appealing, assuring, and intelligent. She was certainly unlike her mother and brother. Acting with his usual impulsiveness, he forgot his previous resolution, and before he left had engaged to begin his occupation of the room on the following day.

The next afternoon found him installed. Yet, after he had unpacked his modest possessions and put them away, after he had placed his few books on the shelves, where they looked glaringly trivial and frivolous beside the late tenant's severe studies ; after he had set out his scanty treasures in the way of photographs and some curious mementoes of his wandering life, and then quickly put them back again with a sudden angry pride at exposing them to the unsympathetic incongruity of the other ornaments, he, nevertheless, felt ill at ease. He glanced in vain around the pretty room. It was not the delicately flowered wall-paper; it was not the white and blue muslin window-curtains gracefully tied up with blue and white ribbons; it was not the spotless bed, with its blue and white festooned mosquito-net and flounced valances, and its medallion portrait of an unknown bishop at the back; it was not the few tastefully framed engravings of certain cardinal virtues, "The Rock of Ages," and "The Guardian Angel"; it was not the casts in relief of "Night" and "Morning"; it was certainly not the cosy dimity-covered arm-chairs and sofa, nor yet the clean-swept polished grate with its cheerful fire sparkling against the chill afternoon sea-fogs without; neither was it the mere feminine suggestion, for that touched a sympathetic chord in his impulsive nature; nor the religious and ascetic influence, for he had occupied a monastic cell in a school of the padres at an old mission, and slept profoundly; — it was none of those, and yet a

part of all. Most habitations retain a cast
or shell of their previous tenant that, fitting
tightly or loosely, is still able to adjust itself
to the newcomer; in most occupied apartments there is still a shadowy suggestion of
the owner's individuality; there was nothing
here that fitted Bly — nor was there either,
strange to say, any evidence of the past proprietor in this inhospitality of sensation. It
did not strike him at the time that it was
this very *lack* of individuality which made it
weird and unreal, that it was strange only
because it was *artificial*, and that a *real*
Tappington had never inhabited it.

He walked to the window — that never-
failing resource of the unquiet mind — and
looked out. He was a little surprised to
find, that, owing to the grading of the house,
the scrub-oaks and bushes of the hill were
nearly on the level of his window, as also
was the adjoining side street on which his
second door actually gave. Opening this,
the sudden invasion of the sea-fog and the
figure of a pedestrian casually passing along
the disused and abandoned pavement not a
dozen feet from where he had been comfortably seated, presented such a striking contrast to the studious quiet and cosiness of his

secluded apartment that he hurriedly closed
the door again with a sense of indiscreet exposure. Returning to the window, he glanced
to the left, and found that he was over-
looked by the side veranda of another villa
in the rear, evidently on its way to take position on the line of the street. Although
in actual and deliberate transit on rollers
across the backyard and still occulting a part
of the view, it remained, after the reckless
fashion of the period, inhabited. Certainly,
with a door fronting a thoroughfare, and a
neighbor gradually approaching him, he
would not feel lonely or lack excitement.

He drew his arm-chair to the fire and
tried to realize the all-pervading yet evasive
Tappington. There was no portrait of him
in the house, and although Mrs. Brooks had
said that he "favored" his sister, Bly had,
without knowing why, instinctively resented
it. He had even timidly asked his employer, and had received the vague reply
that he was "good-looking enough," and the
practical but discomposing retort, "What
do you want to know for?" As he really
did not know why, the inquiry had dropped.
He stared at the monumental crystal ink-
stand half full of ink, yet spotless and free

from stains, that stood on the table, and tried to picture Tappington daintily dipping into it to thank the fair donors — "daughters of Rebecca." Who were they? and what sort of man would they naturally feel grateful to?

What was that?

He turned to the window, which had just resounded to a slight tap or blow, as if something soft had struck it. With an instinctive suspicion of the propinquity of the adjoining street he rose, but a single glance from the window satisfied him that no missile would have reached it from thence. He scanned the low bushes on the level before him; certainly no one could be hiding there. He lifted his eyes toward the house on the left; the curtains of the nearest window appeared to be drawn suddenly at the same moment. Could it have come from there? Looking down upon the window-ledge, there lay the mysterious missile — a little misshapen ball. He opened the window and took it up. It was a small handkerchief tied into a soft knot, and dampened with water to give it the necessary weight as a projectile.

Was it apparently the trick of a mischievous child? or —

But here a faint knock on the door leading into the hall checked his inquiry. He
opened it sharply in his excitement, and was
embarrassed to find the daughter of his hos-
tess standing there, shy, startled, and evidently equally embarrassed by his abrupt
response.

"Mother only wanted me to ask you if
Ellen had put everything to rights," she said,
making a step backwards.

"Oh, thank you. Perfectly," said Herbert with effusion. "Nothing could be
better done. In fact" —

"You're quite sure she hasn't forgotten
anything? or that there isn't anything you
would like changed?" she continued, with
her eyes leveled on the floor.

"Nothing, I assure you," he said, looking
at her downcast lashes. As she still remained motionless, he continued cheerfully,
"Would you — would you — care to look
round and see?"

"No; I thank you."

There was an awkward pause. He still
continued to hold the door open. Suddenly
she moved forward with a school-girl stride,
entered the room, and going to the harmonium, sat down upon the music-stool beside

it, slightly bending forward, with one long, slim, white hand on top of the other, resting over her crossed knees.

Herbert was a little puzzled. It was the awkward and brusque act of a very young person, and yet nothing now could be more gentle and self-composed than her figure and attitude.

"Yes," he continued, smilingly; "I am only afraid that I may not be able to live quite up to the neatness and regularity of the example I find here everywhere. You know I am dreadfully careless and not at all orderly. I shudder to think what may happen ; but you and your mother, Miss Brooks, I trust, will make up your minds to overlook and forgive a good deal. I shall do my best to be worthy of Mr. Tap — of my predecessor — but even then I am afraid you'll find me a great bother."

She raised her shy eyelids. The faintest ghost of a long-buried dimple came into her pale cheek as she said softly, to his utter consternation :

"Rats ! "

Had she uttered an oath he could not have been more startled than he was by this choice gem of Western saloon-slang from the

pure lips of this Evangeline-like figure before him. He sat gazing at her with a wild
hysteric desire to laugh. She lifted her
eyes again, swept him with a slightly terrified glance, and said:

"Tap says you all say that when any one
makes-believe politeness to you."

"Oh, your *brother* says that, does he?"
said Herbert, laughing.

"Yes, and sometimes 'Old rats.' But,"
she continued hurriedly, "*he* does n't say it;
he says *you* all do. My brother is very
particular, and very good. Doctor Stout
loves him. He is thought very much of in
all Christian circles. That book-mark was
given to him by one of his classes."

Every trace of her dimples had vanished.
She looked so sweetly grave, and withal so
maidenly, sitting there slightly smoothing
the lengths of her pink fingers, that Herbert
was somewhat embarrassed.

"But I assure you, Miss Brooks, I was
not making-believe. I am really very careless, and everything is so proper — I mean
so neat and pretty — here, that I " — he
stopped, and, observing the same backward
wandering of her eye as of a filly about to
shy, quickly changed the subject. "You

have, or are about to have, neighbors?" he
said, glancing towards the windows as he
recalled the incident of a moment before.

"Yes; and they're not at all nice people.
They are from Pike County, and very queer.
They came across the plains in '50. They
say 'Stranger'; the men are vulgar, and
the girls very forward. Tap forbids my
ever going to the window and looking at
them. They're quite what you would call
'off color.'"

Herbert, who did not dare to say that he
never would have dreamed of using such an
expression in any young girl's presence, was
plunged in silent consternation.

"Then your brother does n't approve of
them?" he said, at last, awkwardly.

"Oh, not at all. He even talked of having ground-glass put in all these windows,
only it would make the light bad."

Herbert felt very embarrassed. If the
mysterious missile came from these objectionable young persons, it was evidently because they thought they had detected a more
accessible and sympathizing individual in the
stranger who now occupied the room. He
concluded he had better not say anything
about it.

Miss Brooks's golden eyelashes were bent towards the floor. " Do you play sacred music, Mr. Bly ? " she said, without raising them.

" I am afraid not."

" Perhaps you know only negro-minstrel songs ? "

" I am afraid — yes."

" I know one." The dimples faintly came back again. " It 's called ' The Ham-fat Man.' Some day when mother is n't in I 'll play it for you."

Then the dimples fled again, and she immediately looked so distressed that Herbert came to her assistance.

" I suppose your brother taught you that too ? "

" Oh dear, no ! " she returned, with her frightened glance ; " I only heard him say some people preferred that kind of thing to sacred music, and one day I saw a copy of it in a music-store window in Clay Street, and bought it. Oh no ! Tappington did n't teach it to me."

In the pleasant discovery that she was at times independent of her brother's perfections, Herbert smiled, and sympathetically drew a step nearer to her. She rose at once, somewhat primly holding back the sides of her skirt, school-girl fashion, with thumb and finger, and her eyes cast down.

"Good afternoon, Mr. Bly."

"Must you go? Good afternoon."

She walked directly to the open door, looking very tall and stately as she did so, but without turning towards him. When she reached it she lifted her eyes; there was the slightest suggestion of a return of her dimples in the relaxation of her grave little mouth. Then she said, "Good-bye, Mr. Bly," and departed.

The skirt of her dress rustled for an instant in the passage. Herbert looked after her. "I wonder if she skipped then — she looks like a girl that might skip at such a time," he said to himself. "How very odd she is — and how simple! But I must pull her up in that slang when I know her better. Fancy her brother telling her *that!* What a pair they must be!" Nevertheless, when he turned back into the room again he forbore going to the window to indulge further curiosity in regard to his wicked neighbors. A certain new feeling of respect to his late companion — and possibly to himself — held him in check. Much as he resented Tap-

pington's perfections, he resented quite as
warmly the presumption that he was not
quite as perfect, which was implied in that
mysterious overture.   He glanced at the
stool on which she had been sitting with a
half-brotherly smile, and put it reverently on
one side with a very vivid recollection of her
shy maidenly figure.   In some mysterious
way too the room seemed to have lost its
formal strangeness ; perhaps it was the
touch of individuality — *hers* — that had
been wanting ?   He began thoughtfully to
dress himself for his regular dinner at the
Poodle Dog Restaurant, and when he left
the room he turned back to look once more
at the stool where she had sat.   Even on his
way to that fast and famous café of the
period he felt, for the first time in his thought-
less but lonely life, the gentle security of the
home he had left behind him.

II.

IT was three or four days before he became firmly adjusted to his new quarters.
During this time he had met Cherry casually on the staircase, in going or coming, and
received her shy greetings ; but she had not

repeated her visit, nor again alluded to it.
He had spent part of a formal evening in
the parlor in company with a calling deacon,
who, unappalled by the Indian shawl for
which the widow had exchanged her household cerements on such occasions, appeared
to Herbert to have remote matrimonial de-
signs, as far at least as a sympathetic deprecation of the vanities of the present, an
echoing of her sighs like a modest encore, a
preternatural gentility of manner, a vague
allusion to the necessity of bearing "one another's burdens," and an everlasting "promise" in store, would seem to imply. To
Herbert's vivid imagination, a discussion on
the doctrinal points of last Sabbath's ser-
mon was fraught with delicate suggestion ;
and an acceptance by the widow of an appointment to attend the Wednesday evening
"Lectures" had all the shy reluctant yield-
ing of a granted rendezvous. Oddly enough,
the more formal attitude seemed to be reserved for the young people, who, in the suggestive atmosphere of this spiritual flirtation, alone appeared to preserve the propri-
eties and, to some extent, decorously chap-
eron their elders. Herbert gravely turned
the leaves of Cherry's music while she played

and sang one or two discreet but depressing songs expressive of her unalterable but proper devotion to her mother's clock, her father's arm-chair, and her aunt's Bible; and Herbert joined somewhat boyishly in the soul-subduing refrain. Only once he ventured to suggest in a whisper that he would like to add *her* music-stool to the adorable inventory; but he was met by such a disturbed and terrified look that he desisted. "Another night of this wild and reckless dissipation will finish me," he said lugubriously to himself when he reached the solitude of his room. "I wonder how many times a week I'd have to help the girl play the spiritual gooseberry downstairs before we could have any fun ourselves?"

Here the sound of distant laughter, interspersed with vivacious feminine shrieks, came through the open window. He glanced between the curtains. His neighbor's house was brilliantly lit, and the shadows of a few romping figures were chasing each other across the muslin shades of the windows. The objectionable young women were evidently enjoying themselves. In some conditions of the mind there is a certain exasperation in the spectacle of unmeaning enjoyment, and

he shut the window sharply. At the same
moment some one knocked at his door.

It was Miss Brooks, who had just come
upstairs.

" Will you please let me have my music-
stool ? "

He stared at her a moment in surprise,
then recovering himself, said, " Yes, certainly," and brought the stool. For an instant he was tempted to ask why she wanted
it, but his pride forbade him.

" Thank you. Good-night."

" Good-night ! "

" I hope it was n't in your way ? "

" Not at all."

" Good-night ! "

" Good-night."

She vanished. Herbert was perplexed.
Between young ladies whose naïve exuber-
ance impelled them to throw handkerchiefs
at his window and young ladies whose equally
naïve modesty demanded the withdrawal
from his bedroom of a chair on which they
had once sat, his lot seemed to have fallen
in a troubled locality. Yet a day or two
later he heard Cherry practising on the harmonium as he was ascending the stairs on
his return from business ; she had departed

before he entered the room, but had left the music-stool behind her. It was not again removed.

One Sunday, the second or third of his tenancy, when Cherry and her mother were at church, and he had finished some work that he had brought from the bank, his former restlessness and sense of strangeness returned. The regular afternoon fog had thickened early, and, driving him back from a cheerless, chilly ramble on the hill, had left him still more depressed and solitary. In sheer desperation he moved some of the furniture, and changed the disposition of several smaller ornaments. Growing bolder, he even attacked the sacred shelf devoted to Tappington's serious literature and moral studies. At first glance the book of sermons looked suspiciously fresh and new for a volume of habitual reference, but its leaves were carefully cut, and contained one or two book-marks. It was only another evidence of that perfect youth's care and neatness. As he was replacing it he noticed a small object folded in white paper at the back of the shelf. To put the book back into its former position it was necessary to take this out. He did so, but its contents slid

from his fingers and the paper to the floor.
To his utter consternation, looking down he
saw a pack of playing - cards strewn at his
feet !

He hurriedly picked them up. They were
worn and slippery from use, and exhaled a
faint odor of tobacco. Had they been left
there by some temporary visitor unknown to
Tappington and his family, or had they been
hastily hidden by a servant ? Yet they were
of a make and texture superior to those that
a servant would possess ; looking at them
carefully, he recognized them to be of a quality used by the better-class gamblers. Re-
storing them carefully to their former position, he was tempted to take out the other
volumes, and was rewarded with the further
discovery of a small box of ivory counters,
known as "poker-chips." It was really
very extraordinary ! It was quite the *cache*
of some habitual gambler. Herbert smiled
grimly at the irreverent incongruity of the
hiding-place selected by its unknown and
mysterious owner, and amused himself by
fancying the horror of his sainted predecessor had *he* made the discovery. He determined to replace them, and to put some mark
upon the volumes before them in order to

detect any future disturbance of them in his absence.

Ought he not to take Miss Brooks in his confidence? Or should he say nothing about it at present, and trust to chance to discover the sacrilegious hider? Could it possibly be Cherry herself, guilty of the same innocent curiosity that had impelled her to buy the "Ham-fat Man"? Preposterous! Besides, the cards had been used, and she could not play poker alone!

He watched the rolling fog extinguish the line of Russian Hill, the last bit of far perspective from his window. He glanced at his neighbor's veranda, already dripping with moisture; the windows were blank; he remembered to have heard the girls giggling in passing down the side street on their way to church, and had noticed from behind his own curtains that one was rather pretty. This led him to think of Cherry again, and to recall the quaint yet melancholy grace of her figure as she sat on the stool opposite. Why had she withdrawn it so abruptly; did she consider his jesting allusion to it indecorous and presuming? Had he really meant it seriously; and was he beginning to think too much about her? Would she

ever come again? How nice it would be if
she returned from church alone early, and
they could have a comfortable chat together
here! Would she sing the "Ham-fat Man"
for him? Would the dimples come back if
she did? Should he ever know more of this
quaint repressed side of her nature? After
all, what a dear, graceful, tantalizing, lova-
ble creature she was! Ought he not at all
hazards try to know her better? Might it
not be here that he would find a perfect real-
ization of his boyish dreams, and in *her* all
that — what nonsense he was thinking!

Suddenly Herbert was startled by the
sound of a light but hurried foot upon the
wooden outer step of his second door, and
the quick but ineffective turning of the door-
handle. He started to his feet, his mind still
filled with a vision of Cherry. Then he as
suddenly remembered that he had locked the
door on going out, putting the key in his
overcoat pocket. He had returned by the
front door, and his overcoat was now hanging in the lower hall.

The door again rattled impetuously. Then
it was supplemented by a female voice in a
hurried whisper: "Open quick, can't you?
do hurry!"

He was confounded. The voice was au-
thoritative, not unmusical; but it was *not*
Cherry's. Nevertheless he called out quickly,
" One moment, please, and I'll get the key!"
dashed downstairs and up again, breathlessly
unlocked the door and threw it open.

Nobody was there!

He ran out into the street. On one side
it terminated abruptly on the cliff on which
his dwelling was perched; on the other, it
descended more gradually into the next
thoroughfare; but up and down the street,
on either hand, no one was to be seen. A
slightly superstitious feeling for an instant
crept over him. Then he reflected that the
mysterious visitor could in the interval of
his getting the key have easily slipped down
the steps of the cliff or entered the shrub-
bery of one of the adjacent houses. But why
had she not waited? And what did she
want? As he reëntered his door he mechanically raised his eyes to the windows of his
neighbor's. This time he certainly was not
mistaken. The two amused, mischievous
faces that suddenly disappeared behind the
curtain as he looked up showed that the incident had not been unwitnessed. Yet it was
impossible that it could have been either of

them. Their house was only accessible by a
long détour. It might have been the trick
of a confederate; but the tone of half familiarity and half entreaty in the unseen visit-
or's voice dispelled the idea of any collusion.
He entered the room and closed the door
angrily. A grim smile stole over his face as
he glanced around at the dainty saint-like
appointments of the absent Tappington, and
thought what that irreproachable young man
would have said to the indecorous intrusion,
even though it had been a mistake. Would
those shameless Pike County girls have
dared to laugh at *him?*

But he was again puzzled to know why he
himself should have been selected for this
singular experience. Why was *he* considered fair game for these girls? And, for
the matter of that, now that he reflected
upon it, why had even this gentle, refined,
and melancholy Cherry thought it necessary
to talk slang to *him* on their first acquaintance, and offer to sing him the "Ham-fat
Man"? It was true he had been a little
gay, but never dissipated. Of course he
was not a saint, like Tappington — oh, *that*
was it! He believed he understood it now.
He was suffering from that extravagant con-

ception of what worldliness consists of, so common to very good people with no knowledge of the world. Compared to Tappington he was in their eyes, of course, a rake and a roué. The explanation pleased him. He would not keep it to himself. He would gain Cherry's confidence and enlist her sympathies. Her gentle nature would revolt at this injustice to their lonely lodger. She would see that there were degrees of goodness besides her brother's. She would perhaps sit on that stool again and *not* sing the "Ham-fat Man."

A day or two afterwards the opportunity seemed offered to him. As he was coming home and ascending the long hilly street, his eye was taken by a tall graceful figure just preceding him. It was she. He had never before seen her in the street, and was now struck with her ladylike bearing and the grave superiority of her perfectly simple attire. In a thoroughfare haunted by handsome women and striking toilettes, the refined grace of her mourning costume, and a certain stateliness that gave her the look of a young widow, was a contrast that evidently attracted others than himself. It was with an odd mingling of pride and jealousy that

he watched the admiring yet respectful
glances of the passers-by, some of whom
turned to look again, and one or two to re-
trace their steps and follow her at a decorous distance. This caused him to quicken
his own pace, with a new anxiety and a remorseful sense of wasted opportunity. What
a booby he had been, not to have made more
of his contiguity to this charming girl — to
have been frightened at the naïve decorum
of her maidenly instincts! He reached her
side, and raised his hat with a trepidation at
her new-found graces — with a boldness that
was defiant of her other admirers. She
blushed slightly.

"I thought you'd overtake me before,"
she said naïvely. "*I* saw *you* ever so long
ago."

He stammered, with an equal simplicity,
that he had not dared to.

She looked a little frightened again, and
then said hurriedly: "I only thought that
I would meet you on Montgomery Street,
and we would walk home together. I don't
like to go out alone, and mother cannot always go with me. Tappington never cared
to take me out — I don't know why. I think
he did n't like the people staring and stop-

ping us. But they stare more — don't you think? — when one is alone. So I thought if you were coming straight home we might come together — unless you have something else to do?"

Herbert impulsively reiterated his joy at meeting her, and averred that no other engagement, either of business or pleasure, could or would stand in his way. Looking up, however, it was with some consternation that he saw they were already within a block of the house.

"Suppose we take a turn around the hill and come back by the old street down the steps?" he suggested earnestly.

The next moment he regretted it. The frightened look returned to her eyes; her face became melancholy and formal again.

"No!" she said quickly. "That would be taking a walk with you like these young girls and their young men on Saturdays. That's what Ellen does with the butcher's boy on Sundays. Tappington often used to meet them. Doing the 'Come, Philanders,' as he says you call it."

It struck Herbert that the didactic Tappington's method of inculcating a horror of slang in his sister's breast was open to some

objection; but they were already on the
steps of their house, and he was too much
mortified at the reception of his last unhappy suggestion to make the confidential
disclosure he had intended, even if there had
still been time.

"There's mother waiting for me," she
said, after an awkward pause, pointing to
the figure of Mrs. Brooks dimly outlined on
the veranda. "I suppose she was beginning to be worried about my being out alone.
She'll be so glad I met you." It didn't
appear to Herbert, however, that Mrs.
Brooks exhibited any extravagant joy over
the occurrence, and she almost instantly retired with her daughter into the sitting-room,
linking her arm in Cherry's, and, as it were,
empanoplying her with her own invulnerable
shawl. Herbert went to his room more dis-
satisfied with himself than ever.

Two or three days elapsed without his seeing Cherry ; even the well-known rustle of
her skirt in the passage was missing. On
the third evening he resolved to bear the
formal terrors of the drawing-room again,
and stumbled upon a decorous party consist-
ing of Mrs. Brooks, the deacon, and the pas-
tor's wife — but not Cherry. It struck him

on entering that the momentary awkwardness of the company and the formal beginning of a new topic indicated that *he* had
been the subject of their previous conversation. In this idea he continued, through that
vague spirit of opposition which attacks impulsive people in such circumstances, to generally disagree with them on all subjects,
and to exaggerate what he chose to believe
they thought objectionable in him. He did
not remain long; but learned in that brief
interval that Cherry had gone to visit a
friend in Contra Costa, and would be absent
a fortnight; and he was conscious that the
information was conveyed to him with a
peculiar significance.

The result of which was only to intensify
his interest in the absent Cherry, and for a
week to plunge him in a sea of conflicting
doubts and resolutions. At one time he
thought seriously of demanding an explanation from Mrs. Brooks, and of confiding to
her — as he had intended to do to Cherry —
his fears that his character had been misin-
terpreted, and his reasons for believing so.
But here he was met by the difficulty of
formulating what he wished to have explained, and some doubts as to whether his

confidences were prudent. At another time
he contemplated a serious imitation of Tappington's perfections, a renunciation of the
world, and an entire change in his habits.
He would go regularly to church — *her*
church, and take up Tappington's desolate
Bible-class. But here the torturing doubt
arose whether a young lady who betrayed a
certain secular curiosity, and who had evidently depended upon her brother for a
knowledge of the world, would entirely like
it. At times he thought of giving up the
room and abandoning for ever this doubly
dangerous proximity ; but here again he was
deterred by the difficulty of giving a satisfactory reason to his employer, who had procured it as a favor. His passion — for such
he began to fear it to be — led him once to
the extravagance of asking a day's holiday
from the bank, which he vaguely spent in
the streets of Oakland in the hope of accidentally meeting the exiled Cherry.

III.

THE fortnight slowly passed. She returned, but he did not see her. She was always out or engaged in her room with some

female friend when Herbert was at home. This was singular, as she had never appeared to him as a young girl who was fond of visiting or had ever affected female friendships. In fact, there was little doubt now that, wittingly or unwittingly, she was avoiding him.

He was moodily sitting by the fire one evening, having returned early from dinner. In reply to his habitual but affectedly careless inquiry, Ellen had told him that Mrs. Brooks was confined to her room by a slight headache, and that Miss Brooks was out. He was trying to read, and listening to the wind that occasionally rattled the casement and caused the solitary gas-lamp that was visible in the side street to flicker and leap wildly. Suddenly he heard the same footfall upon his outer step and a light tap at the door. Determined this time to solve the mystery, he sprang to his feet and ran to the door; but to his anger and astonishment it was locked and the key was gone. Yet he was positive that *he* had not taken it out.

The tap was timidly repeated. In desperation he called out, "Please don't go away yet. The key is gone; but I'll find it in a moment." Nevertheless he was at his wits' end.

There was a hesitating pause and then the sound of a key cautiously thrust into the lock. It turned; the door opened, and a tall figure, whose face and form were completely hidden in a veil and long gray shawl, quickly glided into the room and closed the door behind it. Then it suddenly raised its arms, the shawl was parted, the veil fell aside, and Cherry stood before him!

Her face was quite pale. Her eyes, usually downcast, frightened, or coldly clear, were bright and beautiful with excitement. The dimples were faintly there, although the smile was sad and half hysterical. She remained standing, erect and tall, her arms dropped at her side, holding the veil and shawl that still depended from her shoulders.

"So — I 've caught you!" she said, with a strange little laugh. "Oh yes. 'Please don't go away yet. I 'll get the key in a moment,'" she continued, mimicking his recent utterance.

He could only stammer, "Miss Brooks — then it was *you?*"

"Yes; and you thought it was *she*, did n't you? Well, and you 're caught! I did n't believe it; I would n't believe it when they said it. I determined to find it out myself. And I have; and it's true."

Unable to determine whether she was serious or jesting, and conscious only of his delight at seeing her again, he advanced impulsively. But her expression instantly changed : she became at once stiff and school-girlishly formal, and stepped back towards the door.

"Don't come near me, or I'll go," she said quickly, with her hand upon the lock.

"But not before you tell me what you mean," he said half laughingly half earnestly. "Who is *she?* and what would n't you have believed? For upon my honor, Miss Brooks, I don't know what you are talking about."

His evident frankness and truthful manner appeared to puzzle her. "You mean to say you were expecting no one?" she said sharply.

"I assure you I was not."

"And — and no woman was ever here — at that door?"

He hesitated. "Not to-night — not for a long time; not since you returned from Oakland."

"Then there *was* one?"

"I believe so."

" You *believe* — you don't *know ?* "

" I believed it was a woman from her voice ; for the door was locked, and the key was downstairs. When I fetched it and opened the door, she — or whoever it was — was gone."

" And that's why you said so imploringly, just now, ' Please don't go away yet' ? You see I 've caught you. Ah ! I don't wonder you blush ! "

If he had, his cheeks had caught fire from her brilliant eyes and the extravagantly affected sternness — as of a school-girl monitor — in her animated face. Certainly he had never seen such a transformation.

" Yes ; but, you see, I wanted to know who the intruder was," he said, smiling at his own embarrassment.

" You did — well, perhaps *that* will tell you ? It was found under your door before I went away." She suddenly produced from her pocket a folded paper and handed it to him. It was a misspelt scrawl, and ran as follows : —

" Why are you so cruel ? Why do you keep me dansing on the stepps before them gurls at the windows ? Was it that stuck-up Saint, Miss Brooks, that you were afraid

of, my deer? Oh, you faithless trater!
Wait till I ketch you! I'll tear your eyes
out and hern!"

It did not require great penetration for
Herbert to be instantly convinced that the
writer of this vulgar epistle and the owner
of the unknown voice were two very different individuals. The note was evidently a
trick. A suspicion of its perpetrators flashed
upon him.

"Whoever the woman was, it was not she
who wrote the note," he said positively.
"Somebody must have seen her at the door.
I remember now that those girls — your
neighbors — were watching me from their
window when I came out. Depend upon it,
that letter comes from them."

Cherry's eyes opened widely with a sudden childlike perception, and then shyly
dropped. "Yes," she said slowly; "they *did*
watch you. They know it, for it was they
who made it the talk of the neighborhood,
and that's how it came to mother's ears."
She stopped, and, with a frightened look,
stepped back towards the door again.

"Then *that* was why your mother" —

"Oh yes," interrupted Cherry quickly.
"That was why I went over to Oakland, and

why mother forbade my walking with you again, and why she had a talk with friends about your conduct, and why she came near telling Mr. Carstone all about it until I stopped her." She checked herself — he could hardly believe his eyes — the pale, nun-like girl was absolutely blushing.

"I thank you, Miss Brooks," he said gravely, "for your thoughtfulness, although I hope I could have still proven my innocence to Mr. Carstone, even if some unknown woman tried my door by mistake, and was seen doing it. But I am pained to think that *you* could have believed me capable of so wanton and absurd an impropriety — and such a gross disrespect to your mother's house."

"But," said Cherry with childlike naïveté, "you know *you* don't think anything of such things, and that's what I told mother."

"You told your mother *that?*"

"Oh yes — I told her Tappington says it's quite common with young men. Please don't laugh — for it's very dreadful. Tappington didn't laugh when he told it to me as a warning. He was shocked."

"But, my dear Miss Brooks" —

"There — now you're angry — and that's

as bad. Are you sure you did n't know that woman?"

"Positive!"

"Yet you seemed very anxious just now that she should wait till you opened the door."

"That was perfectly natural."

"I don't think it was natural at all."

"But — according to Tappington" —

"Because my brother is very good you need not make fun of him."

"I assure you I have no such intention. But what more can I say? I give you my word that I don't know who that unlucky woman was. No doubt she may have been some nearsighted neighbor who had mistaken the house, and I dare say was as thoroughly astonished at my voice as I was at hers. Can I say more? Is it necessary for me to swear that since I have been here no woman has ever entered that door — but " —

"But who?"

"Yourself."

"I know what you mean," she said hurriedly, with her old frightened look, gliding to the outer door. "It 's shameful what I 've done. But I only did it because — because I had faith in you, and did n't be-

lieve what they said was true." She had already turned the lock. There were tears in
her pretty eyes.

"Stop," said Herbert gently. He walked
slowly towards her, and within reach of her
frightened figure stopped with the timid
respect of a mature and genuine passion.
"You must not be seen going out of that
door," he said gravely. "You must let me
go first, and, when I am gone, lock the door
again and go through the hall to your own
room. No one must know that I was in the
house when you came in at that door. Good-
night."

Without offering his hand he lifted his
eyes to her face. The dimples were all
there — and something else. He bowed and
passed out.

Ten minutes later he ostentatiously returned to the house by the front door, and
proceeded up the stairs to his own room. As
he cast a glance around he saw that the
music-stool had been moved before the fire,
evidently with the view of attracting his attention. Lying upon it, carefully folded,
was the veil that she had worn. There could
be no doubt that it was left there purposely.
With a smile at this strange girl's last char-

acteristic act of timid but compromising recklessness, after all his precautions, he raised it tenderly to his lips, and then hastened to hide it from the reach of vulgar eyes. But had Cherry known that its temporary resting-place that night was under his pillow she might have doubted his superior caution.

When he returned from the bank the next afternoon, Cherry rapped ostentatiously at his door. " Mother wishes me to ask you," she began with a certain prim formality, which nevertheless did not preclude dimples, " if you would give us the pleasure of your company at our Church Festival to-night? There will be a concert and a collation. You could accompany us there if you cared. Our friends and Tappington's would be so glad to see you, and Dr. Stout would be delighted to make your acquaintance."

" Certainly ! " said Herbert, delighted and yet astounded. "Then," he added in a lower voice, " your mother no longer believes me so dreadfully culpable ? "

" Oh no," said Cherry in a hurried whisper, glancing up and down the passage ; " I 've been talking to her about it, and she is satisfied that it is all a jealous trick and

slander of these neighbors. Why, I told
her that they had even said that *I* was that
mysterious woman ; that I came that way to
you because she had forbidden my seeing
you openly."

" What ! You dared say that ? "

" Yes ; don't you see ? Suppose they
said they *had* seen me coming in last night
— *that* answers it," she said triumphantly.

" Oh, it does ? " he said vacantly.

" Perfectly. So you see she 's convinced
that she ought to put you on the same foot-
ing as Tappington, before everybody ; and
then there won't be any trouble. You 'll
come, won't you ? It won't be so *very* good.
And then, I 've told mother that as there
have been so many street-fights, and so much
talk about the Vigilance Committee lately, I
ought to have somebody for an escort when
I am coming home. And if you 're known,
you see, as one of *us*, there 'll be no harm in
your meeting me."

" Thank you," he said, extending his hand
gratefully.

Her fingers rested a moment in his.
" Where did you put it ? " she said demurely.

" It ? Oh ! *it 's* all safe," he said quickly,
but somewhat vaguely.

" But I don't call the upper drawer of your bureau safe," she returned poutingly, " where *everybody* can go. So you 'll find it *now* inside the harmonium, on the keyboard."

" Oh, thank you."

" It 's quite natural to have left it there *accidentally* — is n't it ? " she said imploringly, assisted by all her dimples. Alas ! she had forgotten that he was still holding her hand. Consequently, she had not time to snatch it away and vanish, with a stifled little cry, before it had been pressed two or three times to his lips. A little ashamed of his own boldness, Herbert remained for a few moments in the doorway listening, and looking uneasily down the dark passage. Presently a slight sound came over the fanlight of Cherry's room. Could he believe his ears ? The saint-like Cherry — no doubt tutored, for example's sake, by the perfect Tappington — was softly whistling.

In this simple fashion the first pages of this little idyl were quietly turned. The book might have been closed or laid aside even then. But it so chanced that Cherry was an unconscious prophet; and presently it actually became a prudential necessity for her to have a masculine escort when she walked out. For a growing state of lawlessness and crime culminated one day the deep tocsin of the Vigilance Committee, and at its stroke fifty thousand peaceful men, reverting to the first principles of social safety, sprang to arms, assembled at their quarters, or patrolled the streets. In another hour the city of San Francisco was in the hands of a mob — the most peaceful, orderly, well organized, and temperate the world had ever known, and yet in conception as lawless, autocratic, and imperious as the conditions it opposed.

IV.

HERBERT, enrolled in the same section with his employer and one or two fellow-clerks, had participated in the meetings of the committee with the light-heartedness and irresponsibility of youth, regretting only the loss of his usual walk with Cherry and the hours that kept him from her house. He was returning from a protracted meeting one night, when the number of arrests and searching for proscribed and suspected characters had been so large as to induce fears of organized resistance and rescue, and on

reaching the foot of the hill found it already
so late, that to avoid disturbing the family
he resolved to enter his room directly by the
door in the side street. On inserting his
key in the lock it met with some resisting
obstacle, which, however, yielded and apparently dropped on the mat inside. Opening
the door and stepping into the perfectly dark
apartment, he trod upon this object, which
proved to be another key. The family must
have procured it for their convenience during his absence, and after locking the door
had carelessly left it in the lock. It was
lucky that it had yielded so readily.

The fire had gone out. He closed the
door and lit the gas, and after taking off his
overcoat moved to the door leading into the
passage to listen if anybody was still stirring.
To his utter astonishment he found it locked.
What was more remarkable — the key was
also *inside!* An inexplicable feeling took
possession of him. He glanced suddenly
around the room, and then his eye fell upon
the bed. Lying there, stretched at full
length, was the recumbent figure of a man.

He was apparently in the profound sleep
of utter exhaustion. The attitude of his
limbs and the order of his dress — of which

only his collar and cravat had been loosened
— showed that sleep must have overtaken
him almost instantly. In fact, the bed was
scarcely disturbed beyond the actual impress
of his figure. He seemed to be a handsome,
matured man of about forty; his dark
straight hair was a little thinned over the
temples, although his long heavy moustache
was still youthful and virgin. His clothes,
which were elegantly cut and of finer material than that in ordinary use, the delicacy
and neatness of his linen, the whiteness of
his hands, and, more particularly, a certain
dissipated pallor of complexion and lines of
recklessness on the brow and cheek, indicated to Herbert that the man before him
was one of that desperate and suspected
class — some of whose proscribed members
he had been hunting — the professional
gambler!

Possibly the magnetism of Herbert's intent
and astonished gaze affected him. He moved
slightly, half opened his eyes, said "Halloo,
Tap," rubbed them again, wholly opened
them, fixed them with a lazy stare on Herbert, and said:

"Now, who the devil are you?"

"I think *I* have the right to ask that

question, considering that this is my room,"
said Herbert sharply.

" *Your* room ? "

" Yes ! "

The stranger half raised himself on his elbow, glanced round the room, settled himself slowly back on the pillows, with his hands clasped lightly behind his head, dropped his eyelids, smiled, and said :

" Rats ! "

" What ? " demanded Herbert, with a resentful sense of sacrilege to Cherry's virgin slang.

" Well, old rats then ! D' ye think I don't know this shebang ? Look here, Johnny, what are you putting on all this side for, eh ? What 's your little game ? Where 's Tappington ? "

" If you mean Mr. Brooks, the son of this house, who formerly lived in this room," replied Herbert, with a formal precision intended to show a doubt of the stranger's knowledge of Tappington, " you ought to know that he has left town."

" Left town ! " echoed the stranger, raising himself again. " Oh, I see ! getting rather too warm for him here ? Humph ! I ought to have thought of that. Well, you

know, he *did* take mighty big risks, anyway!" He was silent a moment, with his
brows knit and a rather dangerous expression in his handsome face. "So some d—d
hound gave him away — eh?"

"I had n't the pleasure of knowing Mr.
Brooks except by reputation, as the respected son of the lady upon whose house
you have just intruded," said Herbert frig-
idly, yet with a creeping consciousness of
some unpleasant revelation.

The stranger stared at him for a moment,
again looked carefully round the room, and
then suddenly dropped his head back on the
pillow, and with his white hands over his
eyes and mouth tried to restrain a spasm of
silent laughter. After an effort he succeeded,
wiped his moist eyes, and sat up.

"So you did n't know Tappington, eh?"
he said, lazily buttoning his collar.

"No."

"No more do I."

He retied his cravat, yawned, rose, shook
himself perfectly neat again, and going to
Herbert's dressing-table quietly took up a
brush and began to lightly brush himself,
occasionally turning to the window to glance
out. Presently he turned to Herbert and said:

" Well, Johnny, what 's your name ? "

" I am Herbert Bly, of Carstone's Bank."

" So, and a member of this same Vigilance Committee, I reckon," he continued.

" Yes."

" Well, Mr. Bly, I owe you an apology for coming here, and some thanks for the only sleep I 've had in forty-eight hours. I struck this old shebang at about ten o'clock, and it 's now two, so I reckon I 've put in about four hours' square sleep. Now, look here." He beckoned Herbert towards the window. " Do you see those three men standing under that gaslight ? Well, they 're part of a gang of Vigilantes who 've hunted me to the hill, and are waiting to see me come out of the bushes, where they reckon I 'm hiding. Go to them and say that I 'm here ! Tell them you 've got Gentleman George — George Dornton, the man they 've been hunting for a week — in this room. I promise you I won't stir, nor kick up a row, when they 've come. Do it, and Carstone, if he 's a square man, will raise your salary for it, and promote you." He yawned slightly, and then slowly looking around him, drew the easy-chair towards him and dropped comfortably in it, gazing at the astounded and motionless Herbert with a lazy smile.

" You 're wondering what my little game is, Johnny, ain't you ? Well, I 'll tell you. What with being hunted from pillar to post, putting my old pards to no end of trouble, and then slipping up on it whenever I think I 've got a sure thing like this," — he cast an almost affectionate glance at the bed, — " I 've come to the conclusion that it 's played out, and I might as well hand in my checks. It 's only a question of my being *run out* of 'Frisco, or hiding until I can *slip out* myself ; and I 've reckoned I might as well give them the trouble and expense of transportation. And if I can put a good thing in your way in doing it — why, it will sort of make things square with you for the fuss I 've given you."

Even in the stupefaction and helplessness of knowing that the man before him was the notorious duellist and gambler George Dornton, one of the first marked for deportation by the Vigilance Committee, Herbert recognized all he had heard of his invincible coolness, courage, and almost philosophic fatalism. For an instant his youthful imagination checked even his indignation. When he recovered himself, he said, with rising color and boyish vehemence :

" Whoever *you* may be, I am neither a police officer nor a spy. You have no right to insult me by supposing that I would profit by the mistake that made you my guest, or that I would refuse you the sanctuary of the roof that covers your insult as well as your blunder."

The stranger gazed at him with an amused expression, and then rose and stretched out his hand.

" Shake, Mr. Bly ! You 're the only man that ever kicked George Dornton when he deserved it. Good-night ! " He took his hat and walked to the door.

" Stop ! " said Herbert impulsively ; " the night is already far gone ; go back and finish your sleep."

" You mean it ? "

" I do."

The stranger turned, walked back to the bed, unfastening his coat and collar as he did so, and laid himself down in the attitude of a moment before.

" I will call you in the morning," continued Herbert. " By that time," — he hesitated, — " by that time your pursuers may have given up their search. One word more. You will be frank with me ? "

" Go on."

" Tappington and you are — friends ? "

" Well — yes."

" His mother and sister know nothing of this ? "

" I reckon he did n't boast of it. *I* did n't. Is that all ? " sleepily.

" Yes."

" Don't *you* worry about *him*. Good-night."

" Good-night."

But even at that moment George Dornton had dropped off in a quiet, peaceful sleep.

Bly turned down the light, and, drawing his easy-chair to the window, dropped into it in bewildering reflection. This then was the secret — unknown to mother and daughter — unsuspected by all! This was the double life of Tappington, half revealed in his flirtation with the neighbors, in the hidden cards behind the books, in the mysterious visitor — still unaccounted for — and now wholly exploded by this sleeping confederate, for whom, somehow, Herbert felt the greatest sympathy! What was to be done? What should he say to Cherry — to her mother — to Mr. Carstone? Yet he had felt he had done right. From time to time he turned to the motionless recumbent shadow on the bed and listened to its slow and peaceful respiration. Apart from that undefinable attraction which all original natures have for each other, the thrice-blessed mystery of protection of the helpless, for the first time in his life, seemed to dawn upon him through that night.

Nevertheless, the actual dawn came slowly. Twice he nodded and awoke quickly with a start. The third time it was day. The street-lamps were extinguished, and with them the moving, restless watchers seemed also to have vanished. Suddenly a formal deliberate rapping at the door leading to the hall startled him to his feet.

It must be Ellen. So much the better ; he could quickly get rid of her. He glanced at the bed ; Dornton slept on undisturbed. He unlocked the door cautiously, and instinctively fell back before the erect, shawled, and decorous figure of Mrs. Brooks. But an utterly new resolution and excitement had supplanted the habitual resignation of her handsome features, and given them an angry sparkle of expression.

Recollecting himself, he instantly stepped forward into the passage, drawing to the door behind him, as she, with equal celerity, opposed it with her hand.

" Mr. Bly," she said deliberately, " Ellen has just told me that your voice has been heard in conversation with some one in this room late last night. Up to this moment I have foolishly allowed my daughter to persuade me that certain infamous scandals regarding your conduct here were false. I must ask you as a gentleman to let me pass now and satisfy myself."

" But, my dear madam, one moment. Let me first explain — I beg " — stammered Herbert with a half-hysterical laugh. " I assure you a gentleman friend " —

But she had pushed him aside and entered precipitately. With a quick feminine glance round the room she turned to the bed, and then halted in overwhelming confusion.

" It's a friend," said Herbert in a hasty whisper. " A friend of mine who returned with me late, and whom, on account of the disturbed state of the streets, I induced to stay here all night. He was so tired that I have not had the heart to disturb him yet."

" Oh, pray don't ! — I beg " — said Mrs. Brooks with a certain youthful vivacity, but still gazing at the stranger's handsome features as she slowly retreated. "Not for worlds!"

Herbert was relieved; she was actually blushing.

"You see, it was quite unpremeditated, I assure you. We came in together," whispered Herbert, leading her to the door, "and I"—

"Don't believe a word of it, madam," said a lazy voice from the bed, as the stranger leisurely raised himself upright, putting the last finishing touch to his cravat as he shook himself neat again. "I'm an utter stranger to him, and he knows it. He found me here, hiding from the Vigilantes, who were chasing me on the hill. I got in at that door, which happened to be unlocked. He let me stay because he was a gentleman — and — I was n't. I beg your pardon, madam, for having interrupted him before you; but it was a little rough to have him lie on *my* account when he was n't the kind of man to lie on his *own*. You'll forgive him — won't you, please? — and, as I'm taking myself off now, perhaps you'll overlook *my* intrusion too."

It was impossible to convey the lazy

frankness of this speech, the charming smile with which it was accompanied, or the easy yet deferential manner with which, taking up his hat, he bowed to Mrs. Brooks as he advanced toward the door.

"But," said Mrs. Brooks, hurriedly glancing from Herbert to the stranger, "it must be the Vigilantes who are now hanging about the street. Ellen saw them from her window, and thought they were *your* friends, Mr. Bly. This gentleman — your friend" — she had become a little confused in her novel excitement — "really ought not to go out now. It would be madness."

"If you would n't mind his remaining a little longer, it certainly would be safer," said Herbert, with wondering gratitude.

"I certainly should n't consent to his leaving my house now," said Mrs. Brooks with dignity; "and if you would n't mind calling Cherry here, Mr. Bly — she 's in the dining-room — and then showing yourself for a moment in the street and finding out what they wanted, it would be the best thing to do."

Herbert flew downstairs; in a few hurried words he gave the same explanation to the astounded Cherry that he had given to

her mother, with the mischievous addition
that Mrs. Brooks's unjust suspicions had
precipitated her into becoming an amicable
accomplice, and then ran out into the street.
Here he ascertained from one of the Vigilantes, whom he knew, that they were really
seeking Dornton ; but that, concluding that
the fugitive had already escaped to the
wharves, they expected to withdraw their
surveillance at noon. Somewhat relieved,
he hastened back, to find the stranger
calmly seated on the sofa in the parlor with
the same air of frank indifference, lazily
relating the incidents of his flight to the
two women, who were listening with every
expression of sympathy and interest. " Poor
fellow ! " said Cherry, taking the astonished
Bly aside into the hall, " I don't believe he's
half as bad as *they* said he is — or as even
he makes himself out to be. But *did* you
notice mother ? "

Herbert, a little dazed, and, it must be
confessed, a trifle uneasy at this ready acceptance of the stranger, abstractedly said
he had not.

" Why, it's the most ridiculous thing.
She's actually going round *without her
shawl*, and does n't seem to know it."

V.

WHEN Herbert finally reached the bank that morning he was still in a state of doubt and perplexity. He had parted with his grateful visitor, whose safety in a few hours seemed assured, but without the least further revelation or actual allusion to anything antecedent to his selecting Tappington's room as refuge. More than that, Herbert was convinced from his manner that he had no intention of making a confidant of Mrs. Brooks, and this convinced him that Dornton's previous relations with Tappington were not only utterly inconsistent with that young man's decorous reputation, but were unexpected by the family. The stranger's familiar knowledge of the room, his mysterious allusions to the " risks " Tappington had taken, and his sudden silence on the discovery of Bly's ignorance of the whole affair — all pointed to some secret that, innocent or not, was more or less perilous, not only to the son but to the mother and sister. Of the latter's ignorance he had no doubt — but had he any right to enlighten them? Admitting that Tappington had deceived

them with the others, would they thank him
for opening their eyes to it? If they had already a suspicion, would they care to know
that it was shared by him? Halting between his frankness and his delicacy, the
final thought that in his budding relations
with the daughter it might seem a cruel bid
for her confidence, or a revenge for their distrust of him, inclined him to silence. But
an unforeseen occurrence took the matter
from his hands. At noon he was told that
Mr. Carstone wished to see him in his private room!

Satisfied that his complicity with Dornton's escape was discovered, the unfortunate
Herbert presented himself, pale but self-pos-
sessed, before his employer. That brief man
of business bade him be seated, and standing
himself before the fireplace, looked down curiously, but not unkindly, upon his employee.

" Mr. Bly, the bank does not usually interfere with the private affairs of its em-
ployees, but for certain reasons which I pre-
fer to explain to you later, I must ask you
to give me a straightforward answer to one
or two questions. I may say that they have
nothing to do with your relations to the bank,
which are to us perfectly satisfactory."

More than ever convinced that Mr. Carstone was about to speak of his visitor, Herbert signified his willingness to reply.

"You have been seen a great deal with Miss Brooks lately — on the street and elsewhere — acting as her escort, and evidently on terms of intimacy. To do you both justice, neither of you seemed to have made it a secret or avoided observation; but I must ask you directly if it is with her mother's permission?"

Considerably relieved, but wondering what was coming, Herbert answered, with boyish frankness, that it was.

"Are you — engaged to the young lady?"

"No, sir."

"Are you — well, Mr. Bly — briefly, are you what is called 'in love' with her?" asked the banker, with a certain brusque hurrying over of a sentiment evidently incompatible with their present business surroundings.

Herbert blushed. It was the first time he had heard the question voiced, even by himself.

"I am," he said resolutely.

"And you wish to marry her?"

"If I dared ask her to accept a young

man with no position as yet," stammered Herbert.

" People don't usually consider a young man in Carstone's Bank of no position," said the banker dryly ; " and I wish for your sake *that* were the only impediment. For I am compelled to reveal to you a secret." He paused, and folding his arms, looked fixedly down upon his clerk. " Mr. Bly, Tappington Brooks, the brother of your sweetheart, was a defaulter and embezzler from this bank ! "

Herbert sat dumfounded and motionless.

" Understand two things," continued Mr. Carstone quickly. " First, that no purer or better women exist than Miss Brooks and her mother. Secondly, that they know nothing of this, and that only myself and one other man are in possession of the secret."

He slightly changed his position, and went on more deliberately. " Six weeks ago Tappington sat in that chair where you are sitting now, a convicted hypocrite and thief. Luckily for him, although his guilt was plain, and the whole secret of his double life revealed to me, a sum of money advanced in pity by one of his gambling confederates had made his accounts good and saved him from

suspicion in the eyes of his fellow-clerks and
my partners. At first he tried to fight me
on that point; then he blustered and said
his mother could have refunded the money;
and asked me what was a paltry five thousand dollars! I told him, Mr. Bly, that it
might be five years of his youth in state
prison; that it might be five years of sorrow
and shame for his mother and sister; that it
might be an everlasting stain on the name
of his dead father — my friend. He talked
of killing himself: I told him he was a cow-
ardly fool. He asked me to give him up
to the authorities: I told him I intended to
take the law in my own hands and give him
another chance; and then he broke down. I
transferred him that very day, without giving him time to communicate with anybody,
to our branch office at Portland, with a
letter explaining his position to our agent,
and the injunction that for six months he
should be under strict surveillance. I myself undertook to explain his sudden depart-
ure to Mrs. Brooks, and obliged him to write
to her from time to time." He paused, and
then continued : " So far I believe my plan
has been successful: the secret has been
kept; he has broken with the evil associates

that ruined him here — to the best of my
knowledge he has had no communication
with them since; even a certain woman here
who shared his vicious hidden life has abandoned him."

"Are you sure?" asked Herbert involuntarily, as he recalled his mysterious visitor.

"I believe the Vigilance Committee has
considered it a public duty to deport her and
her confederates beyond the State," returned
Carstone dryly.

Another idea flashed upon Herbert.
"And the gambler who advanced the money
to save Tappington?" he said breathlessly.

"Wasn't such a hound as the rest of his
kind, if report says true," answered Carstone.   "He was well known here as George
Dornton — Gentleman George — a man capable of better things.   But he was before
your time, Mr. Bly — *you* don't know him."

Herbert didn't deem it a felicitous moment to correct his employer, and Mr. Carstone continued: "I have now told you
what I thought it was my duty to tell you.
I must leave *you* to judge how far it affects
your relations with Miss Brooks."

Herbert did not hesitate.   "I should be
very sorry, sir, to seem to undervalue your

consideration or disregard your warning; but I am afraid that even if you had been less merciful to Tappington, and he were now a convicted felon, I should change neither my feelings nor my intentions to his sister."

" And you would still marry her?" said Carstone.sternly; " *you*, an employee of the bank, would set the example of allying yourself with one who had robbed it?"

" I — am afraid I would, sir," said Herbert slowly.

" Even if it were a question of your remaining here?" said Carstone grimly.

Poor Herbert already saw himself dismissed and again taking up his weary quest for employment; but, nevertheless, he answered stoutly:

" Yes, sir."

" And nothing will prevent you marrying Miss Brooks?"

"Nothing — save my inability to support her."

" Then," said Mr. Carstone, with a peculiar light in his eyes, " it only remains for the bank to mark its opinion of your conduct by *increasing your salary to enable you to do so!* Shake hands, Mr. Bly," he

said, laughing. " I think you 'll do to tie
to — and I believe the young lady will be of
the same opinion. But not a word to either
her or her mother in regard to what you
have heard. And now I may tell you something more. I am not without hope of Tappington's future, nor — d—n it ! — without
some excuse for his fault, sir. He was arti-
ficially brought up. When my old friend
died, Mrs. Brooks, still a handsome woman,
like all her sex would n't rest until she had
another devotion, and wrapped herself and
her children up in the Church. Theology
may be all right for grown people, but it's
apt to make children artificial; and Tappington was pious before he was fairly good.
He drew on a religious credit before he had
a moral capital behind it. He was brought
up with no knowledge of the world, and
when he went into it — it captured him. I
don't say there are not saints born into the
world occasionally ; but for every one you 'll
find a lot of promiscuous human nature.
My old friend Josh Brooks had a heap of
it, and it would n't be strange if some was
left in his children, and burst through their
straight-lacing in a queer way. That 's all !
Good-morning, Mr. Bly. Forget what I 've

told you for six months, and then I should n't
wonder if Tappington was on hand to give
his sister away."

. . . .

Mr. Carstone's prophecy was but half
realized. At the end of six months Herbert Bly's discretion and devotion were duly
rewarded by Cherry's hand. But Tappington did *not* give her away. That saintly
prodigal passed his period of probation with
exemplary rectitude, but, either from a dread
of old temptation, or some unexplained reason, he preferred to remain in Portland, and
his fastidious nest on Telegraph Hill knew
him no more. The key of the little door
on the side street passed, naturally, into the
keeping of Mrs. Bly.

Whether the secret of Tappington's
double life was ever revealed to the two
women is not known to the chronicler. Mrs.
Bly is reported to have said that the climate
of Oregon was more suited to her brother's
delicate constitution than the damp fogs of
San Francisco, and that his tastes were always opposed to the mere frivolity of metro-
politan society. The only possible reason for
supposing that the mother may have become
cognizant of her son's youthful errors was in

the occasional visits to the house of the handsome George Dornton, who, in the social
revolution that followed the brief reign of
the Vigilance Committee, characteristically
returned as a dashing stockbroker, and the
fact that Mrs. Brooks seemed to have dis-
carded her ascetic shawl forever.   But as all
this was contemporaneous with the absurd
rumor, that owing to the loneliness induced
by the marriage of her daughter she contemplated a similar change in her own condition, it is deemed unworthy the serious consideration of this veracious chronicle.

CAPTAIN JIM'S FRIEND.

I.

HARDLY one of us, I think, really believed
in the auriferous probabilities of Eureka
Gulch. Following a little stream, we had
had one day drifted into it, very much as we
imagined the river gold might have done in
remoter ages, with the difference that *we* remained there, while the river gold to all appearances had not. At first it was tacitly
agreed to ignore this fact, and we made the
most of the charming locality, with its rare
watercourse that lost itself in tangled depths
of manzanita and alder, its laurel-choked
pass, its flower-strewn hillside, and its sum-
mit crested with rocking pines.

"You see," said the optimistic Rowley,
" water 's the main thing after all. If we
happen to strike river gold, thar 's the stream
for washing it; if we happen to drop into
quartz — and that thar rock looks mighty

likely — thar ain't a more natural-born site for a mill than that right bank, with water enough to run fifty stamps. That hillside is an original dump for your tailings, and a ready found inclined road for your trucks, fresh from the hands of Providence; and that road we 're kalkilatin' to build to the turnpike will run just easy along that ridge."

Later, when we were forced to accept the fact that finding gold was really the primary object of a gold-mining company, we still remained there, excusing our youthful laziness and incertitude by brilliant and effective sarcasms upon the unremunerative attractions of the gulch. Nevertheless, when Captain Jim, returning one day from the nearest settlement and post-office, twenty miles away, burst upon us with " Well, the hull thing 'll be settled now, boys ; Lacy Bassett is coming down yer to look round," we felt considerably relieved.

And yet, perhaps, we had as little reason for it as we had for remaining there. There was no warrant for any belief in the special divining power of the unknown Lacy Bassett, except Captain Jim's extravagant faith in his general superiority, and even that had always been a source of amused skepticism to the camp. We were already impatiently familiar with the opinions of this unseen oracle ; he was always impending in Captain Jim's speech as a fragrant memory or an unquestioned authority. When Captain Jim began, " Ez Lacy was one day tellin' me," or, " Ez Lacy Bassett allows," or more formally, when strangers were present, " Ez a partickler friend o' mine, Lacy Bassett — maybe ez you know him — sez," the youthful and lighter members of the Eureka Mining Company glanced at each other in furtive enjoyment. Nevertheless no one looked more eagerly forward to the arrival of this apocryphal sage than these indolent skeptics. It was at least an excitement ; they were equally ready to accept his condemnation of the locality or his justification of their original selection.

He came. He was received by the Eureka Mining Company lying on their backs on the grassy site of the prospective quartz mill, not far from the equally hypothetical " slide " to the gulch. He came by the future stage road — at present a thickset jungle of scrub-oaks and ferns. He was accompanied by Captain Jim, who had gone to meet him on the trail, and for a few moments all critical inspection of himself was withheld by the extraordinary effect he seemed to have upon the faculties of his introducer.

Anything like the absolute prepossession of Captain Jim by this stranger we had never imagined. He approached us running a little ahead of his guest, and now and then returning assuringly to his side with the expression of a devoted Newfoundland dog, which in fluffiness he generally resembled. And now, even after the introduction was over, when he made a point of standing aside in an affectation of carelessness, with his hands in his pockets, the simulation was so apparent, and his consciousness and absorption in his friend so obvious, that it was a relief to us to recall him into the conversation.

As to our own first impressions of the stranger, they were probably correct. We all disliked him; we thought him conceited, self-opinionated, selfish, and untrustworthy. But later, reflecting that this was possibly the result of Captain Jim's over-praise, and finding none of these qualities as yet offensively opposed to our own selfishness and conceit, we were induced, like many others, to forget our first impressions. We could easily correct him if he attempted to impose upon *us*, as he evidently had upon Captain Jim. Believing, after the fashion of most humanity, that there was something about *us* particularly awe-inspiring and edifying to vice or weakness of any kind, we good-humoredly yielded to the cheap fascination of this showy, self-saturated, over-dressed, and underbred stranger. Even the epithet of " blower " as applied to him by Rowley had its mitigations ; in that Trajan community a bully was not necessarily a coward, nor florid demonstration always a weakness.

His condemnation of the gulch was sweeping, original, and striking. He laughed to scorn our half-hearted theory of a gold deposit in the bed and bars of our favorite stream. We were not to look for auriferous alluvium in the bed of any present existing stream, but in the " cement " or dried-up bed of the original prehistoric rivers that formerly ran parallel with the present bed, and which — he demonstrated with the stem of Pickney's pipe in the red dust — could be found by sinking shafts at right angles with the stream. The theory was to us, at that time, novel and attractive. It was true that the scientific explanation, although full and gratuitous, sounded vague and incoherent. It was true that the geological terms were not always correct, and their pronunciation defective, but we accepted such extraordinary discoveries as " ignus fatuus rock," " splendiferous drift," " mica twist " (recalling a popular species of tobacco), " iron pirates," and " discomposed quartz " as part of what he not inaptly called a " tautological formation," and were happy. Nor was our contentment marred by the fact that the well-known scientific authority with whom the stranger had been intimate, — to the point of " sleeping together " during a survey, — and whom he described as a bent old man with spectacles, must have aged considerably since one of our party saw him three years before as a keen young fellow of twenty-five. Inaccuracies like those were only the carelessness of genius. " That's my opinion, gentlemen," he concluded, negligently rising, and with pointed preoccupation whipping the dust of Eureka Gulch from his clothes with his handkerchief, " but of course it ain't nothin' to me."

Captain Jim, who had followed every word with deep and trustful absorption, here repeated, " It ain't nothing to him, boys,"

with a confidential implication of the gratuitous blessing we had received, and then
added, with loyal encouragement to him, " It
ain't nothing to you, Lacy, in course," and
laid his hand on his shoulder with infinite
tenderness.

We, however, endeavored to make it something to Mr. Lacy Bassett. · He was spon-
taneously offered a share in the company
and a part of Captain Jim's tent. He accepted both after a few deprecating and
muttered asides to Captain Jim, which the
latter afterwards explained to us was the
giving up of several other important enter-
prises for our sake. When he finally
strolled away with Rowley to look over the
gulch, Captain Jim reluctantly tore himself
away from him only for the pleasure of reit-
erating his praise to us as if in strictest confidence and as an entirely novel proceeding.

" You see, boys, I did n't like to say it
afore *him*, we bein' old friends; but, between us, that young feller ez worth thou-
sands to the camp. Mebbee," he continued
with grave naïveté, " I ain't said much about
him afore, mebbee, bein' old friends and accustomed to him — you know how it is, boys,
— I have n't appreciated him as much ez

I ought, and ez you do. In fact, I don't ezakly remember how I kem to ask him down yer. It came to me suddent, one day only a week ago Friday night, thar under that buckeye; I was thinkin' o' one of his sayins, and sez I — thar 's Lacy, if he was here he 'd set the hull thing right. It was the ghost of a chance my findin' him free, but I did. And there *he* is, and yer *we* are settled! Ye noticed how he just knocked the bottom outer our plans to work. Ye noticed that quick sort o' sneerin' smile o' his, did n't ye — that 's Lacy! I 've seen him knock over a heap o' things without sayin' anythin' — with jist that smile."

It occurred to us that we might have some difficulty in utilizing this smile in our present affairs, and that we should have probably preferred something more assuring, but Captain Jim's faith was contagious.

"What is he, anyway?" asked Joe Walker lazily.

"Eh!" echoed Captain Jim in astonishment. "What is Lacy Bassett?"

"Yes, what is he?" repeated Walker.

"Wot *is* — he?"

"Yes."

"I 've knowed him now goin' as four

year," said Captain Jim with slow reflective contentment. " Let 's see. It was in the fall o' '54 I first met him, and he 's allus been the same ez you see him now."

" But what is his business or profession ? What does he do ? "

Captain Jim looked reproachfully at his questioner.

" Do ? " he repeated, turning to the rest of us as if disdaining a direct reply. " Do ? — why, wot he 's doin' now. He 's allus the same, allus Lacy Bassett."

Howbeit, we went to work the next day under the superintendence of the stranger with youthful and enthusiastic energy, and began the sinking of a shaft at once. To do Captain Jim's friend justice, for the first few weeks he did not shirk a fair share of the actual labor, replacing his objectionable and unsuitable finery with a suit of serviceable working clothes got together by general contribution of the camp, and assuring us of a fact we afterwards had cause to remember, that " he brought nothing but himself into Eureka Gulch." It may be added that he certainly had not brought money there, as Captain Jim advanced the small amounts necessary for his purchases in the distant settlement, and for the still smaller sums he lost at cards, which he played with characteristic self-sufficiency.

Meantime the work in the shaft progressed slowly but regularly. Even when the novelty had worn off and the excitement of anticipation grew fainter, I am afraid that we clung to this new form of occupation as an apology for remaining there; for the fascinations of our vagabond and unconventional life were more potent than we dreamed of. We were slowly fettered by our very freedom; there was a strange spell in this very boundlessness of our license that kept us from even the desire of change; in the wild and lawless arms of nature herself we found an embrace as clinging, as hopeless and restraining, as the civilization from which we had fled. We were quite content after a few hours' work in the shaft to lie on our backs on the hillside staring at the unwinking sky, or to wander with a gun through the virgin forest in search of game scarcely less vagabond than ourselves. We indulged in the most extravagant and dreamy speculations of the fortune we should eventually discover in the shaft, and believed that we were practical. We broke our "saleratus

bread " with appetites unimpaired by restlessness or anxiety ; we went to sleep under
the grave and sedate stars with a serene consciousness of having fairly earned our rest ;
we awoke the next morning with unabated
trustfulness, and a sweet obliviousness of
even the hypothetical fortunes we had perhaps won or lost at cards overnight. We
paid no heed to the fact that our little capital was slowly sinking with the shaft, and
that the rainy season — wherein not only
" no man could work," but even such play
as ours was impossible — was momentarily
impending.

In the midst of this, one day Lacy Bassett
suddenly emerged from the shaft before his
" shift " of labor was over with every sign of
disgust and rage in his face and inarticulate
with apparent passion. In vain we gathered
round him in concern ; in vain Captain Jim
regarded him with almost feminine sympathy, as he flung away his pick and dashed
his hat to the ground.

" What's up, Lacy, old pard ? What's
gone o' you ? " said Captain Jim tenderly.

" Look ! " gasped Lacy at last, when every
eye was on him, holding up a small fragment of rock before us and the next moment

grinding it under his heel in rage. "Look! To think that I 've been fooled agin by this blanked fossiliferous trap — blank it! To think that after me and Professor Parker was once caught jist in this way up on the Stanislaus at the bottom of a hundred-foot shaft by this rotten trap — that yer I am — bluffed agin!"

There was a dead silence; we looked at each other blankly.

"But, Bassett," said Walker, picking up a part of the fragment, "we 've been finding this kind of stuff for the last two weeks."

"But how?" returned Lacy, turning upon him almost fiercely. "Did ye find it super-posed on quartz, or did you find it *not* super-posed on quartz? Did you find it in vol-canic drift, or did ye find it in old red-sand-stone or coarse illuvion? Tell me that, and then ye kin talk. But this yer blank fossil-iferous trap, instead o' being superposed on top, is superposed on the bottom. And that means " —

"What?" we all asked eagerly.

"Why — blank it all — that this yer con-vulsion of nature, this prehistoric volcanic earthquake, instead of acting laterally and chuckin' the stream to one side, has been

revolutionary and turned the old river-bed
bottom-side up, and yer d—d cement hez got
half the globe atop of it! Ye might strike
it from China, but nowhere else."

We continued to look at one another, the
older members with darkening faces, the
younger with a strong inclination to laugh.
Captain Jim, who had been concerned only
in his friend's emotion, and who was hanging with undisguised satisfaction on these
final convincing proofs of his superior geological knowledge, murmured approvingly
and confidingly, " He's right, boys! Thar
ain't another man livin' ez could give you
the law and gospil like that! Ye can tie to
what he says. That's Lacy all over."

Two weeks passed. We had gathered,
damp and disconsolate, in the only available
shelter of the camp. For the long summer
had ended unexpectedly to us ; we had one
day found ourselves caught like the improvi-
dent insect of the child's fable with gauzy
and unseasonable wings wet and bedraggled
in the first rains, homeless and hopeless.
The scientific Lacy, who lately spent most
of his time as a bar-room oracle in the settlement, was away, and from our dripping
canvas we could see Captain Jim returning

from a visit to him, slowly plodding along
the trail towards us.

"It's no use, boys," said Rowley, sum-
marizing the result of our conference, "we
must speak out to him, and if nobody else
cares to do it I will. I don't know why we
should be more mealy-mouthed than they are
at the settlement. They don't hesitate to
call Bassett a dead-beat, whatever Captain
Jim says to the contrary."

The unfortunate Captain Jim had halted
irresolutely before the gloomy faces in the
shelter. Whether he felt instinctively some
forewarning of what was coming I cannot
say. There was a certain dog-like consciousness in his eye and a half-backward glance
over his shoulder as if he were not quite certain that Lacy was not following. The rain
had somewhat subdued his characteristic
fluffiness, and he cowered with a kind of
sleek storm-beaten despondency over the
smoking fire of green wood before our tent.

Nevertheless, Rowley opened upon him
with a directness and decision that astonished us. He pointed out briefly that Lacy
Bassett had been known to us only through
Captain Jim's introduction. That he had
been originally invited there on Captain

Jim's own account, and that his later connection with the company had been wholly the
result of Captain Jim's statements. That,
far from being any aid or assistance to them,
Bassett had beguiled them by apocryphal
knowledge and sham scientific theories into an
expensive and gigantic piece of folly. That,
in addition to this, they had just discovered
that he had also been using the credit of the
company for his own individual expenses at
the settlement while they were working on his
d—d fool shaft — all of which had brought
them to the verge of bankruptcy. That, as
a result, they were forced now to demand his
resignation — not only on their general account, but for Captain Jim's sake — believing firmly, as they did, that he had been
as grossly deceived in his friendship for
Lacy Bassett as *they* were in their business
relations with him.

Instead of being mollified by this, Captain
Jim, to our greater astonishment, suddenly
turned upon the speaker, bristling with his
old canine suggestion.

"There! I said so! Go on! I'd have
sworn to it afore you opened your lips. I
knowed it the day you sneaked around and
wanted to know wot his business was! I

said to myself, Cap, look out for that sneakin'
hound Rowley, he's no friend o' Lacy's.
And the day Lacy so far demeaned himself as to give ye that splendid explanation
o' things, I watched ye; ye did n't think
it, but I watched ye. Ye can't fool me! I
saw ye lookin' at Walker there, and I said
to myself, Wot's the use, Lacy, wot's the
use o' your slingin' them words to such as
them? Wot do *they* know? It's just their
pure jealousy and ignorance. Ef you'd
come down yer, and lazed around with us
and fallen into our common ways, you'd ha'
been ez good a man ez the next. But no, it
ain't your style, Lacy, you're accustomed to
high-toned men like Professor Parker, and
you can't help showing it. No wonder you
took to avoidin' us; no wonder I've had to
foller you over the Burnt Wood Crossin'
time and again, to get to see ye. I see it
all now: ye can't stand the kempany I
brought ye to! Ye had to wipe the slum
gullion of Eureka Gulch off your hands,
Lacy" — He stopped, gasped for breath, and
then lifted his voice more savagely, "And
now, what's this? Wot's this hogwash?
this yer lyin' slander about his gettin' things
on the kempany's credit? Eh, speak up,
some of ye!"

We were so utterly shocked and stupefied
at the degradation of this sudden and unexpected outburst from a man usually so honorable, gentle, self-sacrificing, and forgiving,
that we forgot the cause of it and could only
stare at each other. What was this cheap
stranger, with his shallow swindling tricks,
to the ignoble change he had worked upon
the man before us. Rowley and Walker,
both fearless fighters and quick to resent an
insult, only averted their saddened faces and
turned aside without a word.

" Ye dussen't say it ! Well, hark to me
then," he continued with white and feverish lips. " *I* put him up to helpin' himself.
I told him to use the kempany's name for
credit. Ye kin put that down to *me*. And
when ye talk of *his* resigning, I want ye to
understand that *I* resign outer this rotten
kempany and *take him with me!* Ef all
the gold yer lookin' for was piled up in that
shaft from its bottom in hell to its top in the
gulch, it ain't enough to keep me here away
from him ! Ye kin take all my share — all
my rights yer above ground and below it —
all I carry," — he threw his buckskin purse
and revolver on the ground, — " and pay
yourselves what you reckon you've lost

through *him*. But you and me is quits from to-day."

He strode away before a restraining voice or hand could reach him. His dripping figure seemed to melt into the rain beneath the thickening shadows of the pines, and the next moment he was gone. From that day forward Eureka Gulch knew him no more. And the camp itself somehow melted away during the rainy season, even as he had done.

II.

THREE years had passed. The pioneer stage-coach was sweeping down the long descent to the pastoral valley of Gilead, and I was looking towards the village with some pardonable interest and anxiety. For I carried in my pocket my letters of promotion from the box seat of the coach — where I had performed the functions of treasure messenger for the Excelsior Express Company — to the resident agency of that company in the bucolic hamlet before me. The few dusty right-angled streets, with their rigid and staringly new shops and dwellings, the stern formality of one or two obelisk-like meeting-house spires, the illimitable out-

lying plains of wheat and wild oats beyond,
with their monotony scarcely broken by
skeleton stockades, corrals, and barrack-
looking farm buildings, were all certainly
unlike the unkempt freedom of the mountain
fastnesses in which I had lately lived and
moved. Yuba Bill, the driver, whose usual
expression of humorous discontent deepened
into scorn as he gathered up his reins as if
to charge the village and recklessly sweep it
from his path, indicated a huge, rambling,
obtrusively glazed, and capital-lettered building with a contemptuous flick of his whip as
we passed. " Ef you 're kalkilatin' we 'll
get our partin' drink there you 're mistaken.
That 's wot they call a *temperance house* —
wot means a place where the licker ye get
underhand is only a trifle worse than the
hash ye get above - board. I suppose it 's
part o' one o' the mysteries o' Providence
that wharever you find a dusty hole like this
— that 's naturally *thirsty* — ye run agin a
' temperance ' house. But never *you* mind !
I should n't wonder if thar was a demijohn
o' whiskey in the closet of your back office,
kept thar by the feller you 're relievin' —
who was a white man and knew the ropes."

A few minutes later, when my brief in-

stallation was over, we *did* find the demijohn in the place indicated. As Yuba Bill
wiped his mouth with the back of his heavy
buckskin glove, he turned to me not unkindly. "I don't like to set ye agin Gil-
e-ad, which is a scrip-too-rural place, and a
God-fearin' place, and a nice dry place, and
a place ez I 've heard tell whar they grow
beans and pertatoes and garden sass ; but
afore three weeks is over, old pard, you 'll
be howlin' to get back on that box seat with
me, whar you uster sit, and be ready to take
your chances agin, like a little man, to get
drilled through with buckshot from road
agents. You hear me! I 'll give you three
weeks, sonny, just three weeks, to get your
butes full o' hayseed and straws in yer har ;
and I 'll find ye wadin' the North Fork at
high water to get out o' this." He shook
my hand with grim tenderness, removing his
glove — a rare favor — to give me the pres-
sure of his large, soft, protecting palm, and
strode away. The next moment he was
shaking the white dust of Gilead from his
scornful chariot-wheels.

In the hope of familiarizing myself with
the local interests of the community, I took
up a copy of the " Gilead Guardian " which

lay on my desk, forgetting for the moment
the usual custom of the country press to dis-
place local news for long editorials on for-
eign subjects and national politics. I found,
to my disappointment, that the "Guardian"
exhibited more than the usual dearth of domestic intelligence, although it was singularly oracular on "The State of Europe,"
and "Jeffersonian Democracy." A certain
cheap assurance, a copy-book dogmatism, a
colloquial familiarity, even in the impersonal
plural, and a series of inaccuracies and blunders here and there, struck some old chord
in my memory. I was mutely wondering
where and when I had become personally
familiar with rhetoric like that, when the
door of the office opened and a man entered.
I was surprised to recognize Captain Jim.

I had not seen him since he had indignantly left us, three years before, in Eureka
Gulch. The circumstances of his defection
were certainly not conducive to any volun-
tary renewal of friendship on either side;
and although, even as a former member of
the Eureka Mining Company, I was not conscious of retaining any sense of injury, yet
the whole occurrence flashed back upon me
with awkward distinctness. To my relief,

however, he greeted me with his old cordiality; to my amusement he added to it a
suggestion of the large forgiveness of conscious rectitude and amiable toleration. I
thought, however, I detected, as he glanced
at the paper which was still in my hand and
then back again at my face, the same uneasy
canine resemblance I remembered of old. He
had changed but little in appearance; perhaps he was a trifle stouter, more mature,
and slower in his movements. If I may
return to my canine illustration, his grayer,
dustier, and more wiry *ensemble* gave me
the impression that certain pastoral and agricultural conditions had varied his type, and
he looked more like a shepherd's dog in
whose brown eyes there was an abiding consciousness of the care of straying sheep, and
possibly of one black one in particular.

He had, he told me, abandoned mining
and taken up farming on a rather large
scale. He had prospered. He had other
interests at stake, "A flour-mill with some
improvements — and — and "— here his eyes
wandered to the "Guardian" again, and
he asked me somewhat abruptly what I
thought of the paper. Something impelled
me to restrain my previous fuller criticism,

and I contented myself by saying briefly
that I thought it rather ambitious for the
locality. "That's the word," he said with
a look of gratified relief, "'ambitious' —
you've just hit it. And what's the matter
with thet? Ye kan't expect a high-toned
man to write down to the level of every kar-
pin' hound, ken ye now? That's what he
says to me " — He stopped half confused,
and then added abruptly: "That's one o'
my investments."

"Why, Captain Jim, I never suspected
that you " —

"Oh, I don't *write* it," he interrupted
hastily. "I only furnish the money and the
advertising, and run it gin'rally, you know;
and I'm responsible for it. And I select
the eddyter — and " — he continued, with a
return of the same uneasy wistful look —
"thar's suthin' in thet, you know, eh?"

I was beginning to be perplexed. The
memory evoked by the style of the editorial
writing and the presence of Captain Jim
was assuming a suspicious relationship to
each other. "And who's your editor?" I
asked.

"Oh, he's — he's — er — Lacy Bassett,"
he replied, blinking his eyes with a hopeless

assumption of carelessness. "Let's see! Oh yes! You knowed Lacy down there at Eureka. I disremembered it till now. Yes, sir!" he repeated suddenly and almost rudely, as if to preclude any adverse criticism, "he's the eddyter!"

To my surprise he was quite white and tremulous with nervousness. I was very sorry for him, and as I really cared very little for the half-forgotten escapade of his friend except so far as it seemed to render *him* sensitive, I shook his hand again heartily and began to talk of our old life in the gulch — avoiding as far as possible any allusion to Lacy Bassett. His face brightened; his old simple cordiality and trustfulness returned, but unfortunately with it his old disposition to refer to Bassett. "Yes, they waz high old times, and ez I waz sayin' to Lacy on'y yesterday, there is a kind o' freedom 'bout that sort o' life that runs civilization and noospapers mighty hard, however high-toned they is. Not but what Lacy ain't right," he added quickly, "when he sez that the opposition the 'Guardian' gets here comes from ignorant low-down fellers ez wos brought up in played-out camps, and can't tell a gentleman and a scholar and a scientific man when they sees him. No! So I sez to Lacy, 'Never you mind, it's high time they did, and they've got to do it and to swaller the "Guardian," if I sink double the money I 've already put into the paper.'"

I was not long in discovering from other sources that the "Guardian" was not popular with the more intelligent readers of Gilead, and that Captain Jim's extravagant estimate of his friend was by no means indorsed by the community. But criticism took a humorous turn even in that practical settlement, and it appeared that Lacy Bassett's vanity, assumption, and ignorance were an unfailing and weekly joy to the critical, in spite of the vague distrust they induced in the more homely-witted, and the dull acquiescence of that minority who accepted the paper for its respectable exterior and advertisements. I was somewhat grieved, however, to find that Captain Jim shared equally with his friend in this general verdict of incompetency, and that some of the most outrageous blunders were put down to *him*. But I was not prepared to believe that Lacy had directly or by innuendo helped the public to this opinion.

Whether through accident or design on

his part, Lacy Bassett did not personally obtrude himself upon my remembrance until a month later. One dazzling afternoon, when the dust and heat had driven the pride of Gilead's manhood into the surreptitious shadows of the temperance hotel's back room, and had even cleared the express office of its loungers, and left me alone with darkened windows in the private office, the outer door opened and Captain Jim's friend entered as part of that garish glitter I had shut out. To do the scamp strict justice, however, he was somewhat subdued in his dress and manner, and, possibly through some gentle chastening of epigram and revolver since I had seen him last, was less aggressive and exaggerated. I had the impression, from certain odors wafted through the apartment and a peculiar physical exaltation that was inconsistent with his evident moral hesitancy, that he had prepared himself for the interview by a previous visit to the hidden fountains of the temperance hotel.

"We don't seem to have run agin each other since you 've been here," he said with an assurance that was nevertheless a trifle forced, " but I reckon we 're both busy men,

and there's a heap too much loafing goin' on
in Gilead. Captain Jim told me he met you
the day you arrived; said you just cottoned
to the 'Guardian' at once and thought
it a deal too good for Gilead; eh? Oh,
well, jest ez likely he *did n't* say it — it was
only his gassin'. He's a queer man — is
Captain Jim."

I replied somewhat sharply that I considered him a very honest man, a very simple
man, and a very loyal man.

"That's all very well," said Bassett, twirling his cane with a patronizing smile, "but,
as his friend, don't you find him considerable of a darned fool?"

I could not help retorting that I thought
he had found that hardly an objection.

"*You* think so," he said querulously, apparently ignoring everything but the practical
fact, — "and maybe others do; but that's
where you're mistaken. It don't pay. It
may pay *him* to be runnin' me as his particular friend, to be quotin' me here and there,
to be gettin' credit of knowin' me and my
friends and ownin' me — by Gosh! but I
don't see where the benefit to *me* comes in.
Eh? Take your own case down there at
Eureka Gulch; did n't he send for me just to

show me up to you fellers? Did I want to
have anything to do with the Eureka Company? Did n't he set me up to give my opinion about that shaft just to show off what
I knew about science and all that? And
what did he get me to join the company for?
Was it for you? No! Was it for me?
No! It was just to keep me there for *himself*, and kinder pit me agin you fellers and
crow over you! Now that ain't my style!
It may be *his* — it may be honest and simple and loyal, as you say, and it may be all
right for him to get me to run up accounts
at the settlement and then throw off on me
— but it ain't my style. I suppose he let
on that I did that. No? He did n't?
Well then, why did he want to run me off
with him, and cut the whole concern in an
underhand way and make me leave with
nary a character behind me, eh? Now, I
never said anything about this before — did
I? It ain't like me. I would n't have
said anything about it now, only you talked
about *my* being benefited by his darned
foolishness. Much I 've made outer *him*."

Despicable, false, and disloyal as this
was, perhaps it was the crowning meanness
of such confidences that his very weakness

seemed only a reflection of Captain Jim's own, and appeared in some strange way to degrade his friend as much as himself. The simplicity of his vanity and selfishness was only equalled by the simplicity of Captain Jim's admiration of it. It was a part of my youthful inexperience of humanity that I was not above the common fallacy of believing that a man is " known by the company he keeps," and that he is in a manner responsible for its weakness; it was a part of that humanity that I felt no surprise in being more amused than shocked by this revelation. It seemed a good joke on Captain Jim!

" Of course *you* kin laugh at his darned foolishness; but, by Gosh, it ain't a laughing matter to me!"

" But surely he's given you a good position on the ' Guardian,' " I urged. " That was disinterested, certainly."

" Was it? I call that the cheekiest thing yet. When he found he could n't make enough of me in private life, he totes me out in public as *his* editor — the man who runs *his* paper! And has his name in print as the proprietor, the only chance he 'd ever get of being before the public. And don't know the whole town is laughing at him! "

"That may be because they think *he* writes some of the articles," I suggested.

Again the insinuation glanced harmlessly from his vanity. "That could n't be, because *I* do all the work, and it ain't his style," he said with naïve discontent. "And it's always the highest style, done to please him, though between you and me it's sorter castin' pearls before swine — this 'Frisco editing — and the public would be just as satisfied with anything I could rattle off that was peart and sassy, — something spicy or personal. I'm willing to climb down and do it, for there's nothin' stuck-up about me, you know; but that darned fool Captain Jim has got the big head about the style of the paper, and darned if I don't think he's afraid if there's a lettin' down, people may think it's him! Ez if! Why, you know as well as me that there's a sort of snap *I* could give these things that would show it was me and no slouch did them, in a minute."

I had my doubts about the elegance or playfulness of Mr. Bassett's trifling, but from some paragraphs that appeared in the next issue of the "Guardian" I judged that he had won over Captain Jim — if indeed that gentleman's alleged objections were not

entirely the outcome of Bassett's fancy. The
social paragraphs themselves were clumsy
and vulgar. A dull-witted account of a
select party at Parson Baxter's, with a point-
blank compliment to Polly Baxter his daughter, might have made her pretty cheek burn
but for her evident prepossession for the
meretricious scamp, its writer. But even
this horse-play seemed more natural than
the utterly artificial editorials with their
pinchbeck glitter and cheap erudition; and
thus far it appeared harmless.

I grieve to say that these appearances
were deceptive. One afternoon, as I was returning from a business visit to the outskirts
of the village, I was amazed on reëntering
the main street to find a crowd collected
around the "Guardian" office, gazing at the
broken glass of its windows and a quantity
of type scattered on the ground. But my
attention was at that moment more urgently
attracted by a similar group around my own
office, who, however, seemed more cautious,
and were holding timorously aloof from the
entrance. As I ran rapidly towards them, a
few called out, "Look out — he's in there!"
while others made way to let me pass. With
the impression of fire or robbery in my mind,

I entered precipitately, only to find Yuba Bill calmly leaning back in an arm-chair with his feet on the back of another, a glass of whiskey from my demijohn in one hand and a huge cigar in his mouth. Across his lap lay a stumpy shotgun which I at once recognized as " the Left Bower," whose usual place was at his feet on the box during his journeys. He looked cool and collected, although there were one or two splashes of printer's ink on his shirt and trousers, and from the appearance of my lavatory and towel he had evidently been removing similar stains from his hands. Putting his gun aside and grasping my hand warmly without rising, he began with even more than his usual lazy imperturbability:

" Well, how 's Gilead lookin' to-day ? "

It struck me as looking rather disturbed, but, as I was still too bewildered to reply, he continued lazily:

" Ez you did n't hunt me up, I allowed you might hev got kinder petrified and dried up down yer, and I reckoned to run down and rattle round a bit and make things lively for ye. I 've jist cleared out a newspaper office over thar. They call it the 'Guardi-an,' though it did n't seem to offer much pertection to them fellers ez was in it. In fact, it was n't ez much a fight ez it orter hev been. It was rather monotonous for me."

"But what's the row, Bill? What has happened?" I asked excitedly.

"Nothin' to speak of, I tell ye," replied Yuba Bill reflectively. "I jest meandered into that shop over there, and I sez, 'I want ter see the man ez runs this yer mill o' literatoor an' progress.' Thar waz two infants sittin' on high chairs havin' some innocent little game o' pickin' pieces o' lead outer pill-boxes like, and as soon ez they seed me one of 'em crawled under his desk and the other scooted outer the back door. Bimeby the door opens again, and a fluffy coyote-lookin' feller comes in and allows that *he* is responsible for that yer paper. When I saw the kind of animal he was, and that he had n't any weppings, I jist laid the Left Bower down on the floor. Then I sez, 'You allowed in your paper that I oughter hev a little sevility knocked inter me, and I 'm here to hev it done. You ken begin it now.' With that I reached for him, and we waltzed oncet or twicet around the room, and then I put him up on the mantelpiece and on them desks and

little boxes, and took him down again, and
kinder wiped the floor with him gin'rally,
until the first thing I knowed he was outside
the winder on the sidewalk. On'y blamed
if I did n't forget to open the winder. Ef
it had n't been for that, it would hev been
all quiet and peaceful-like, and nobody hev
knowed it. But the sash being in the way,
it sorter created a disturbance and unpleas-
antness *outside.*"

"But what was it all about?" I repeated.
"What had he done to you?"

"Ye 'll find it in that paper," he said, indicating a copy of the "Guardian" that lay
on my table with a lazy nod of his head.
"P'r'aps you don't read it? No more do I.
But Joe Bilson sez to me yesterday: ' Bill,'
sez he, ' they 're goin' for ye in the "Guardian."' 'Wot 's that?' sez I. 'Hark to
this,' sez he, and reads out that bit that
you 'll find there."

I had opened the paper, and he pointed
to a paragraph. "There it is. Pooty, ain't
it?" I read with amazement as follows : —

"If the Pioneer Stage Company want to
keep up with the times, and not degenerate into
the old style ' one hoss ' road-wagon business,
they 'd better make some reform on the line.

They might begin by shipping off some of the old-time whiskey-guzzling drivers who are too high and mighty to do anything but handle the ribbons, and are above speaking to a passenger unless he's a favorite or one of their set. Over-praise for an occasional scrimmage with road agents, and flattery from Eastern greenhorns, have given them the big head. If the fool-killer were let loose on the line with a big club, and knocked a little civility into their heads, it would n't be a bad thing, and would be a parti-cular relief to the passengers for Gilead who have to take the stage from Simpson's Bar."

"That's my stage," said Yuba Bill quietly, when I had ended ; " and that's *me*."

"But it's impossible," I said eagerly. "That insult was never written by Captain Jim."

"Captain Jim," repeated Yuba Bill re-flectively. "Captain Jim, — yes, that was the name o' the man I was playin' with. Shortish hairy feller, suthin' between a big coyote and the old-style hair-trunk. Fought pretty well for a hay - footed man from Gil-e-ad."

"But you 've whipped the wrong man, Bill," I said. "Think again! Have you had any quarrel lately?— run against any newspaper man?" The recollection had flashed upon me that Lacy Bassett had lately returned from a visit to Stockton.

Yuba Bill regarded his boots on the other arm-chair for a few moments in profound meditation. "There was a sort o' gaudy insect," he began presently, "suthin' half-way betwixt a hoss-fly and a devil's darnin'-needle, ez crawled up onter the box seat with me last week, and buzzed! Now I think on it, he talked high-faluten' o' the inflooence of the press and sech. I may hev said 'shoo' to him when he was hummin' the loudest. I mout hev flicked him off oncet or twicet with my whip. It must be him. Gosh!" he said suddenly, rising and lifting his heavy hand to his forehead, "now I think agin *he was the feller ez crawled under the desk when the fight was goin' on, and stayed there.* Yes, sir, that was *him*. His face looked sorter familiar, but I did n't know him moultin' with his feathers off." He turned upon me with the first expression of trouble and anxiety I had ever seen him wear. "Yes, sir, that 's him. And I 've kem — me, Yuba Bill! — kem *myself*, a matter of twenty miles, totin' a *gun* — a gun, by Gosh! — to fight that — that — that potatar-bug!" He walked to the window, turned, walked back again, finished his whiskey with a single gulp, and laid his hand almost despondingly on my shoulder. " Look ye, old — old fell, you and me 's ole friends. Don't give me away. Don't let on a word o' this to any one! Say I kem down yer howlin' drunk on a gen'ral tear! Say I mistook that newspaper office for a cigar-shop, and — got licked by the boss! Say anythin' you like, 'cept that I took a gun down yer to chase a fly that had settled onter me. Keep the Left Bower in yer back office till I send for it. Ef you 've got a back door somewhere handy where I can slip outer this without bein' seen I 'd be thankful."

As this desponding suggestion appeared to me as the wisest thing for him to do in the then threatening state of affairs outside, — which, had he suspected it, he would have stayed to face, — I quickly opened a door into a courtyard that communicated through an alley with a side street. Here we shook hands and parted; his last dejected ejaculation being, " That potato-bug!" Later I ascertained that Captain Jim had retired to his ranch some four miles distant. He was not seriously hurt, but looked, to use the words of my informant, "ez ef he 'd been hugged by a playful b'ar." As the "Guardian" made its appearance the next week without the slightest allusion to the fracas, I did not deem it necessary to divulge the real facts. When I called to inquire about Captain Jim's condition, he himself, however, volunteered an explanation.

"I don't mind tellin' you, ez an old friend o' mine and Lacy's, that the secret of that there attack on me and the 'Guardian' was perlitikal. Yes, sir! There was a powerful orginization in the interest o' Halkins for assemblyman ez did n't like our high-toned editorials on caucus corruption, and hired a bully to kem down here and suppress us. Why, this yer Lacy spotted the idea to oncet; yer know how keen he is."

"Was Lacy present?" I asked as carelessly as I could.

Captain Jim glanced his eyes over his shoulder quite in his old furtive canine fashion, and then blinked them at me rapidly. "He war! And if it warn't for *his* pluck and *his* science and *his* strength, I don't know whar *I'd* hev been now! Howsom-

ever, it's all right. I've had a fair offer to
sell the 'Guardian' over at Simpson's Bar,
and it's time I quit throwin' away the work
of a man like Lacy Bassett upon it. And
between you and me, I've got an idea and
suthin' better to put his talens into."

III.

It was not long before it became evident
that the "talens" of Mr. Lacy Bassett, as
indicated by Captain Jim, were to grasp at
a seat in the state legislature. An editorial in the "Simpson's Bar Clarion" boldly
advocated his pretensions. At first it was
believed that the article emanated from the
gifted pen of Lacy himself, but the style
was so unmistakably that of Colonel Star-
bottle, an eminent political " war-horse " of
the district, that a graver truth was at once
suggested, namely, that the " Guardian "
had simply been transferred to Simpson's
Bar, and merged into the " Clarion " solely
on this condition. At least it was recognized that it was the hand of Captain Jim
which guided the editorial fingers of the
colonel, and Captain Jim's money that dis-
tended the pockets of that gallant political
leader.

Howbeit Lacy Bassett was never elected; in fact he was only for one brief moment a candidate. It was related that upon his first ascending the platform at Simpson's Bar a voice in the audience said lazily, " Come down ! " That voice was Yuba Bill's. A slight confusion ensued, in which Yuba Bill whispered a few words in the colonel's ear. After a moment's hesitation the " war-horse " came forward, and in his loftiest manner regretted that the candidate had withdrawn. The next issue of the " Clarion " proclaimed with no uncertain sound that a base conspiracy gotten up by the former proprietor of the " Guardian " to undermine the prestige of the Great Express Company had been ruthlessly exposed, and the candidate on learning it *himself* for the first time, withdrew his name from the canvass, as became a high - toned gentleman. Public opinion, ignoring Lacy Bassett completely, unhesitatingly denounced Captain Jim.

During this period I had paid but little heed to Lacy Bassett's social movements, or the successes which would naturally attend such a character with the susceptible sex. I had heard that he was engaged to Polly Baxter, but that they had quarrelled in conse-

quence of his flirtations with others, especially a Mrs. Sweeny, a profusely ornamented
but reputationless widow. Captain Jim had
often alluded with a certain respectful pride
and delicacy to Polly's ardent appreciation
of his friend, and had more than half hinted
with the same reverential mystery to their
matrimonial union later, and his intention
of " doing the square thing " for the young
couple. But it was presently noticed that
these allusions became less frequent during
Lacy's amorous aberrations, and an occasional depression and unusual reticence
marked Captain Jim's manner when the
subject was discussed in his presence. He
seemed to endeavor to make up for his
friend's defection by a kind of personal hom-
age to Polly, and not unfrequently accompanied her to church or to singing-class. I
have a vivid recollection of meeting him one
afternoon crossing the fields with her, and
looking into her face with that same wistful,
absorbed, and uneasy canine expression that
I had hitherto supposed he had reserved for
Lacy alone. I do not know whether Polly
was averse to the speechless devotion of these
yearning brown eyes; her manner was animated and the pretty cheek that was nearest

me mantled as I passed ; but I was struck
for the first time with the idea that Captain
Jim loved her ! I was surprised to have that
fancy corroborated in the remark of another
wayfarer whom I met, to the effect, "That
now that Bassett was out o' the running it
looked ez if Captain Jim was makin' up for
time ! " Was it possible that Captain Jim
had always loved her ? I did not at first
know whether to be pained or pleased for
his sake. But I concluded that whether the
unworthy Bassett had at last found a *rival*
in Captain Jim or in the girl herself, it was
a displacement that was for Captain Jim's
welfare. But as I was about leaving Gilead
for a month's transfer to the San Francisco
office, I had no opportunity to learn more
from the confidences of Captain Jim.

I was ascending the principal staircase of
my San Francisco hotel one rainy afternoon,
when I was pointedly recalled to Gilead by
the passing glitter of Mrs. Sweeny's jewelry
and the sudden vanishing behind her of a
gentleman who seemed to be accompanying
her. A few moments after I had entered
my room I heard a tap at my door, and
opened it upon Lacy Bassett. I thought
he looked a little confused and agitated.

Nevertheless, with an assumption of cordiality and ease he said, " It appears we 're neighbors. That 's my room next to yours." He pointed to the next room, which I then remembered was a sitting-room *en suite* with my own, and communicating with it by a second door, which was always locked. It had not been occupied since my tenancy. As I suppose my face did not show any extravagant delight at the news of his contiguity, he added, hastily, " There 's a transom over the door, and I thought I 'd tell you you kin hear everything from the one room to the other."

I thanked him, and told him dryly that, as I had no secrets to divulge and none that I cared to hear, it made no difference to me. As this seemed to increase his confusion and he still hesitated before the door, I asked him if Captain Jim was with him.

" No," he said quickly. " I have n't seen him for a month, and don't want to. Look here, I want to talk to you a bit about him." He walked into the room, and closed the door behind him. " I want to tell you that me and Captain Jim is played ! All this runnin' o' me and interferin' with me is played ! I 'm tired of it. You kin tell him so from me."

"Then you have quarrelled?"

"Yes. As much as any man can quarrel with a darned fool who can't take a hint."

"One moment. Have you quarrelled about Polly Baxter?"

"Yes," he answered querulously. "Of course I have. What does he mean by interfering?"

"Now listen to me, Mr. Bassett," I interrupted. "I have no desire to concern myself in your association with Captain Jim, but since you persist in dragging me into it, you must allow me to speak plainly. From all that I can ascertain you have no serious intentions of marrying Polly Baxter. You have come here from Gilead to follow Mrs. Sweeny, whom I saw you with a moment ago. Now, why do you not frankly give up Miss Baxter to Captain Jim, who will make her a good husband, and go your own way with Mrs. Sweeny? If you really wish to break off your connection with Captain Jim, that 's the only way to do it."

His face, which had exhibited the weakest and most pitiable consciousness at the mention of Mrs. Sweeny, changed to an expression of absolute stupefaction as I concluded.

"Wot stuff are you tryin' to fool me with?" he said at last roughly.

"I mean," I replied sharply, "that this double game of yours is disgraceful. Your association with Mrs. Sweeny demands the withdrawal of any claim you have upon Miss Baxter at once. If you have no respect for Captain Jim's friendship, you must at least show common decency to her."

He burst into a half-relieved, half-hysteric laugh. "Are you crazy?" gasped he. "Why, Captain Jim's just huntin' *me* down to make *me* marry Polly. That's just what the row's about. That's just what he's inter-ferin' for — just to carry out his darned fool ideas o' gettin' a wife for me ; just his vanity to say *he's* made the match. It's *me* that he wants to marry to that Baxter girl — not himself. He's too cursed selfish for that."

I suppose I was not different from ordi-nary humanity, for in my unexpected dis-comfiture I despised Captain Jim quite as much as I did the man before me. Reiterat-ing my remark that I had no desire to mix myself further in their quarrels, I got rid of him with as little ceremony as possible. But a few minutes later, when the farcical side of the situation struck me, my irritation was somewhat mollified, without however in-creasing my respect for either of the actors.

The whole affair had assumed a triviality
that was simply amusing, nothing more, and
I even looked forward to a meeting with
Captain Jim and *his* exposition of the matter — which I knew would follow — with
pleasurable anticipation. But I was mistaken.

One afternoon, when I was watching the
slanting volleys of rain driven by a strong
southwester against the windows of the
hotel reading-room, I was struck by the
erratic movements of a dripping figure outside that seemed to be hesitating over the
entrance to the hotel. At times furtively
penetrating the porch as far as the vestibule,
and again shyly recoiling from it, its manner
was so strongly suggestive of some timid animal that I found myself suddenly reminded
of Captain Jim and the memorable evening
of his exodus from Eureka Gulch. As the
figure chanced to glance up to the window
where I stood I saw to my astonishment that
it *was* Captain Jim himself, but so changed
and haggard that I scarcely knew him. I
instantly ran out into the hall and vestibule,
but when I reached the porch he had disappeared. Either he had seen me and wished
to avoid me, or he had encountered the ob-

ject of his quest, which I at once concluded
must be Lacy Bassett. I was so much impressed and worried by his appearance and
manner, that, in this belief, I overcame my
aversion to meeting Bassett, and even sought
him through the public rooms and lobbies in
the hope of finding Captain Jim with him.
But in vain; possibly he had succeeded in
escaping his relentless friend.

As the wind and rain increased at nightfall and grew into a tempestuous night, with
deserted streets and swollen waterways, I
did not go out again, but retired early, inex-
plicably haunted by the changed and brooding face of Captain Jim. Even in my
dreams he pursued me in his favorite likeness of a wistful, anxious, and uneasy hound,
who, on my turning to caress him familiarly,
snapped at me viciously, and appeared to
have suddenly developed a snarling rabid
fury. I seemed to be awakened at last by
the sound of his voice. For an instant I
believed the delusion a part of my dream.
But I was mistaken; I was lying broad
awake, and the voice clearly had come from
the next room, and was distinctly audible
over the transom.

"I've had enough of it," he said, "and

I'm givin' ye now — this night — yer last chance. Quit this hotel and that woman, and go back to Gilead and marry Polly. Don't do it and I'll kill ye, ez sure ez you sit there gapin' in that chair. If I can't get ye to fight me like a man, — and I'll spit in yer face or put some insult onto you afore that woman, afore everybody, ez would make a bigger skunk nor you turn, — I'll hunt ye down and kill ye in your tracks."

There was a querulous murmur of interruption in Lacy's voice, but whether of defiance or appeal I could not distinguish. Captain Jim's voice again rose, dogged and distinct.

" Ef *you* kill me it's all the same, and I don't say that I won't thank ye. This yer world is too crowded for yer and me, Lacy Bassett. I've believed in ye, trusted in ye, lied for ye, and fought for ye. From the time I took ye up — a feller-passenger to 'Fresco — believin' there wor the makin's of a man in ye, to now, you fooled me, — fooled me afore the Eureka boys; fooled me afore Gilead; fooled me afore *her*; fooled me afore God! It's got to end here. Ye've got to take the curse of that foolishness off o' me! You've got to do one single thing that 's like the man I took ye for, or you 've got to die. Times waz when I 'd have wished it for your account — that 's gone, Lacy Bassett! You 've got to do it for *me*. You 've got to do it so I don't see ' d—d fool ' writ in the eyes of every man ez looks at me."

He had apparently risen and walked towards the door. His voice sounded from another part of the room.

" I 'll give ye till to-morrow mornin' to do suthin' to lift this curse off o' me. Ef you refoose, then, by the living God, I 'll slap yer face in the dinin'-room, or in the office afore them all! You hear me ! "

There was a pause, and then a quick sharp explosion that seemed to fill and expand both rooms until the windows were almost lifted from their casements, a hysterical inarticulate cry from Lacy, the violent opening of a door, hurried voices, and the tramping of many feet in the passage. I sprang out of bed, partly dressed myself, and ran into the hall. But by that time I found a crowd of guests and servants around the next door, some grasping Bassett, who was white and trembling, and others kneeling by Captain Jim, who was half lying in the doorway against the wall.

"He heard it all," Bassett gasped hysterically, pointing to me. "*He* knows that this man wanted to kill me."

Before I could reply, Captain Jim partly raised himself with a convulsive effort. Wiping away the blood that, oozing from his lips, already showed the desperate character of his internal wound, he said in a husky and hurried voice: "It's all right, boys! It's my fault. It was *me* who done it. I went for him in a mean underhanded way jest now, when he had n't a weppin nor any show to defend himself. We gripped. He got a holt o' my derringer — you see that's *my* pistol there, I swear it — and turned it agin me in self-defense, and sarved me right. I swear to God, gentlemen, it's so!" Catching sight of my face, he looked at me, I fancied half imploringly and half triumphantly, and added, "I might hev knowed it! I allers allowed Lacy Bassett was game! — game, gentlemen — and he was. If it's my last word, I say it — he was game!"

And with this devoted falsehood upon his lips and something of the old canine instinct in his failing heart, as his head sank back he seemed to turn it towards Bassett, as if to stretch himself out at his feet. Then the light failed from his yearning upward glance, and the curse of foolishness was lifted from him forever.

So conclusive were the facts, that the coroner's jury did not deem it necessary to detain Mr. Bassett for a single moment after the inquest. But he returned to Gilead, married Polly Baxter, and probably on the strength of having "killed his man," was unopposed on the platform next year, and triumphantly elected to the legislature !

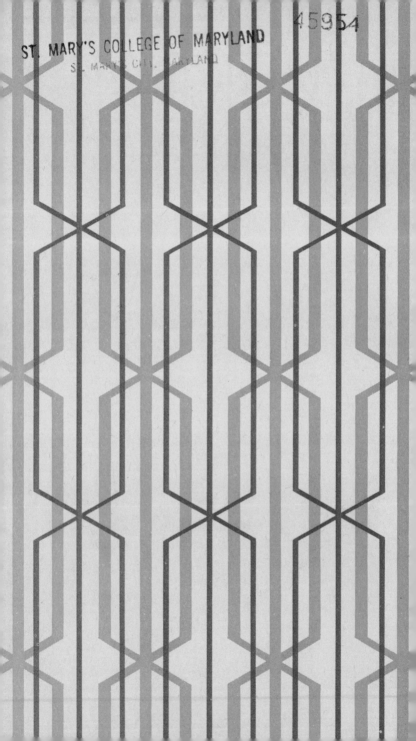